# the Mystery
## of the
# Headless
# Horse

**Alfred Hitchcock**
and The Three Investigators in

# the **Mystery**
## of the
# Headless
# Horse

Text by William Arden

Based on characters created by Robert Arthur

Illustrated by Jack Hearne

Random House  New York

Copyright © 1977 by Random House, Inc.
All rights reserved under International and Pan-American Copyright conventions. Published in the United States by Random House, Inc., New York, and simultaneously in Canada by Random House of Canada Limited, Toronto.

**Library of Congress Cataloging in Publication Data**
——.
Alfred Hitchcock and the three investigators in The mystery of the headless horse.
(Alfred Hitchcock mystery series; 26)
SUMMARY: When three junior detectives search for a valuable old Spanish sword lost since the Mexican War, the headless statue of a horse yields a clue.
(1. Mystery and detective stories)  I. Arthur, Robert.  II. Hearne, Jack.  III. Title.  IV. Title: The mystery of the headless horse.  V. Series.
PZ7.L984Ai                      Fic                      77–74458
ISBN 0–394–83569–7                      ISBN 0–394–93569–1 lib. bdg.

Manufactured in the United States of America          1 2 3 4 5 6 7 8 9 0

# Contents

# Alfred Hitchcock
# presents!

Welcome once again to the world of The Three Investigators, those maddeningly industrious young sleuths whom it is my occasional pleasure to introduce. The lads have just completed a most remarkable and instructive adventure. I think it is quite worthy of your attention.

What could be more remarkable than to solve a mystery dating back to the Mexican War? A mystery that involves a headless horse, a legendary jeweled sword, and a trio of long-forgotten scoundrels whose devious trail must somehow be followed after more than 130 years! And what could be more instructive than to discover that dusty old historical documents do not always tell the truth? At the very least, one must learn to read between the lines!

Such is the nature of the challenging mystery that our young detectives unravel on the following pages. Their efforts are prompted by most praiseworthy motives—an unselfish desire to help the proud and honorable Alvaro family, descendants of the first citizens of California, and a natural thirst for excitement and adventure. In tackling this latest case, the boys again demonstrate the ingenuity and bravery that have made them famous with mystery lovers around the world.

What! You say that you have never even heard of The Three Investigators? Then you must meet them at once!

The leader of the trio is the annoyingly clever Jupiter Jones, whose mental powers are exceeded only by his weight. His companions are Pete Crenshaw, a muscular and merry lad who is inclined to be nervous, and the steady and studious Bob Andrews. All three boys live in the coastal town of Rocky Beach, California, not far from Hollywood. They make their headquarters in an old mobile home trailer hidden in the fabulous Jones Salvage Yard.

So, you are introduced. Now turn the page and follow The Three Investigators into mystery and danger—if you dare!

ALFRED HITCHCOCK

# the Mystery
## of the
# Headless
# Horse

# An angry meeting

"Hey, Jupe! Diego Alvaro wants to talk to you," called Pete Crenshaw as he came out the front door of Rocky Beach Central School. Classes had just finished for the day, and his friends Jupiter Jones and Bob Andrews were already outside waiting for him.

"I didn't know you knew Alvaro," Bob said to Jupiter.

"I don't really," Jupiter replied. "He's in the California History Club with me, but he always keeps pretty much to himself. What does he want, Pete?"

"I don't know. He just asked if you'd meet him at the field gate after school—if you could spare the time. He acted like it was pretty important."

"Perhaps he needs the services of The Three Investigators," Jupe said hopefully. Jupiter, Pete, and Bob were members of a junior detective team, and they hadn't had a case in quite a while.

Pete shrugged. "Maybe. But it's you he wants to see."

"We'll all go meet him," ordered Jupe.

Pete and Bob nodded and fell into step with their over-weight friend. They were used to doing what Jupiter wanted. As the brainy leader of The Three Investigators, Jupe made most of the decisions for the group. Sometimes the other two boys objected. Pete, a tall, athletic boy, hated Jupe's habit of boldly walking into danger while on a case. Bob, a slight, studious youth, admired Jupe's quick intelligence but occasionally flared at his high-handed ways. Still, life was never dull when Jupiter was around. He had an uncanny ability to scent a mystery and find excitement. Most of the time the three boys were the best of friends.

Jupiter now led the way around the corner of the school to a quiet, tree-lined side street. Far down the block was a gate to the school's athletic field. The boys hunched into their windbreakers. It was a Thursday afternoon in November, and although the day was sunny, a chill breeze was blowing up the street.

"I don't see Diego," Bob said, peering through his glasses as the trio neared the field gate.

"But look who else is here!" said Pete with a groan.

Just beyond the field gate a small, open truck was parked. Half pickup truck and half car, it was one of those vehicles called ranch wagons. A broad, burly man in a cowboy hat, denim jacket, blue jeans, and western boots sat on the front fender. Next to him lounged a tall, skinny boy with a long nose. On the truck's door, some elegant gold lettering read "Norris Ranch."

"Skinny Norris!" Bob scowled. "What's he doing—?"

Before Bob could finish what he was saying, the tall boy spotted them and called out:

"Well, if it isn't Fatso Sherlock Holmes and the two dumb bloodhounds!" Skinny laughed nastily.

Skinny—E. Skinner Norris—was an old enemy of The Three Investigators. The spoiled son of a well-to-do businessman, Skinny was always showing off and trying to prove that he was smarter than Jupiter. He always failed, but he managed to make a good deal of trouble for the detectives. He had one advantage over them—he was a few years older and he already had his driver's license and his own sports car. The Investigators envied his mobility as much as they resented his bullying.

Jupiter couldn't ignore Skinny's latest insult. Halting just short of the field gate, he blandly said:

"Did you hear someone speak, Bob?"

"I sure don't see anyone," Bob replied.

"But I sure smell someone." Pete sniffed. "Or something."

The burly cowboy on the truck fender laughed and looked at Skinny. The tall boy reddened. He stepped menacingly toward the Investigators, his fists clenched. He was about to answer when a new voice called out:

"Jupiter Jones! I'm sorry I am late. I would like very much to ask you a favor."

A slim boy with dark hair and dark eyes came out through the field gate. He stood so straight that he seemed taller than he was. He wore narrow old jeans, low riding boots, and a loose white shirt sewn with colorful stitching. He spoke without an accent, but his formal manner suggested his ties to old Spanish customs.

"What kind of favor, Diego?" Jupiter asked.

Skinny Norris laughed. "Hey, you're a buddy of wetbacks now, Fatso? That figures. Why don't you help send him back to Mexico? Do us all a favor."

Diego Alvaro whirled. He moved so swiftly and smoothly that he was standing in front of Skinny before the tall boy had stopped laughing.

"You will take that back," Diego said. "You will apologize."

"A head shorter, younger, and way below Skinny's weight, Diego stood firmly in front of the bigger boy. He looked as dignified as a Spanish don.

"Nuts," Skinny said. "I don't apologize to Mexicans."

Without a word, Diego slapped Skinny's sneering face.
"Why you little—!"

Skinny knocked the smaller boy down. Diego bounced
up instantly and tried to hit Skinny. The big boy knocked
him down again. Diego got up, went down, and got up
again. Skinny stopped grinning. He pushed Diego away
from him, out into the street, and looked around as if he
wanted someone to stop the uneven fight.

"Hey, someone get this little punk—"

Jupiter and Pete started toward them. The burly cowboy, laughing, jumped off the truck fender.

"Okay, Alvaro," the cowboy said. "Cut it out. You'll get
hurt."

"NO!"

Everyone froze. The sharp command came from a man
who seemed to appear from nowhere. He looked like an
older version of Diego. Though much taller, he had the
same slim, compact build and the same dark hair and eyes.
He, too, wore old riding jeans, scuffed western boots, and
a decorated shirt—a faded black one with red and yellow
stitching. On his head was a black sombrero banded with
conchos—circular pieces of silver. His face was haughty,
and his eyes were cold and hard.

"No one will interfere," the newcomer snapped. "It is for
the boys to settle between themselves."

The cowboy shrugged and leaned back against the
ranch wagon. Intimidated by the newcomer's fierceness,
the Investigators could only watch. Skinny glared at them
all and turned to face Diego. In the street, the smaller
boy raised his fists and moved forward.

"Okay, you asked for it!" Skinny snarled, stepping off
the curb.

The two boys grappled with each other in the space be-

tween the ranch wagon and the next parked car. Suddenly Skinny leaped backwards to get more room for a final, crushing blow at Diego.

"Look out!" screamed Bob and Pete together.

Skinny's backward leap had put him directly in the path of an oncoming car! Still watching Diego, Skinny didn't see the danger he was in!

Brakes squealed, but the car would never stop in time!

Diego dove wildly at Skinny and struck him full force with his shoulder, trying to hurl him out of the way of the car. Both boys fell to the pavement as the skidding car passed and screeched to a stop fifteen feet away!

Two still figures lay in the street. The bystanders rushed forward, filled with dread.

Then Diego stirred and slowly got up, smiling. He was untouched! And Skinny was unhurt, too. Diego's tackle had shoved him across the path of the car to safety.

Grinning, Bob and Pete pounded Diego on the back as the driver of the car hurried up to them.

"That was quick thinking, son! Are you all right?"

Diego nodded. The driver thanked him, and made sure that Skinny was unhurt before driving away. Skinny was still lying in the street, pale and shaken.

"Lucky! Darn lucky!" muttered Skinny's cowboy friend as he helped the boy to his feet.

"I . . . I guess he saved me," Skinny said.

"He sure did!" Pete exclaimed. "You better thank him."

Grudgingly, Skinny nodded. "Thanks, Alvaro."

"You thank me?" Diego said. "That's all?"

Skinny looked confused. "What?"

"I have not yet heard an apology," Diego said evenly.

Skinny stared dumbfounded at the slim boy.

"You will take back what you said," Diego demanded.

Skinny flushed. "If it means that much to you, okay, I guess I take it back. I . . ."

"Then I am satisfied," Diego said. He turned his back on Skinny and walked away.

"Hey, now—" Skinny began. Then he saw Bob, Pete, and Jupiter grinning. His narrow face turned red with anger. He hurried toward the ranch wagon. "Cody!" he called to the cowboy. "Let's get out of here!"

The cowboy looked at Diego and the fierce stranger, who now stood beside the boy.

"You two just made yourselves a lot of trouble," Cody said.

Then he got into the ranch wagon beside Skinny and drove away.

# 2

# The Alvaro pride

As Cody's menacing words echoed in their ears, the Three Investigators saw Diego stare after the ranch wagon in dismay.

"My stupid pride!" Diego wailed. "It will ruin us!"

"No, Diego!" the tall stranger snapped. "You did well. For an Alvaro, pride and honor come first always."

Diego turned to the boys. "This is my brother, Pico. He is the head of our family. My brother, these friends are Jupiter Jones, Pete Crenshaw, and Bob Andrews."

Serious and formal, Pico Alvaro bowed to the boys. He was no more than twenty-five, but even in his old jeans, battered boots, and worn black shirt he seemed like some old Spanish nobleman.

"Señores. We are honored that you meet with us."

"*De nada*," Jupiter said, and bowed in return.

"Ah?" Pico smiled. "You speak Spanish, Jupiter?"

"I read it," Jupiter said, a little shamefaced, "but I can't really speak it. At least, not the way you speak English."

"You have no need to speak two languages," said Pico politely. "We are proud of our heritage, so we speak Spanish. But we are Americans, as you are, so English is our language also."

Before Jupe could respond, Pete burst out impatiently, "What did that Cody guy mean when he said you'd made yourselves a lot of trouble?"

"An empty wind without meaning," Pico said scornfully.

Diego said uneasily, "I don't know, Pico. Mr. Norris . . ."

"Do not bother others with our troubles, Diego."

"You do have some trouble?" Jupiter said. "With Cody and Skinny Norris?"

"A trifle of no importance," Pico declared.

"I don't call stealing our ranch a trifle!" Diego said.

Bob and Pete gaped. "Your ranch? How . . . ?"

"Calmly, Diego," Pico said. "Steal is a strong word."

"What word is better?" Jupiter asked.

Pico thought for a moment. "Some months ago, Mr. Norris bought the rancho next to ours. He plans to buy others nearby and have one large ranch—as an investment, I think. He wanted our rancho, but it is all we have, and although he offered a good price we refused to sell. Mr. Norris was quite angry."

"He was mad as a roped stallion," Diego said with a grin.

"You see," Pico continued, "our land contains an old dam and reservoir on Santa Inez Creek. For his large ranch, Mr. Norris needs that water. When we refused to sell, he offered more money. And when we still refused, he tried to prove that our old Spanish land grant wasn't legal. But it is. Our land is ours."

"He even had Cody tell the sheriff our rancho is a fire hazard because we don't have enough men," Diego said angrily.

"Who *is* Cody?" Bob asked.

"Mr. Norris's ranch manager," Pico explained. "Norris is a businessman. He has no knowledge of ranching."

"The sheriff didn't believe your place is a fire hazard?" Pete said. "So your ranch is safe?"

Pico sighed. "We support ourselves, but we have little

money. We fell behind in paying our taxes. Mr. Norris found out, and tried to have the county take over the ranch so he could buy it from them. We had to pay our taxes quickly, so . . ."

"You got a mortgage from a bank," Jupiter guessed.

Pete frowned. "What's a mortgage, Jupe?"

"A loan on a house or land or both," Jupiter explained. "If you don't pay the loan, the bank takes the house or land."

"You mean," Pete said, "you get a loan to pay taxes so the county won't take your ranch, but you have to pay back the loan or the bank takes the ranch! Sounds like out of the frying pan and into the fire, if you ask me."

"No, Jupiter said. "You have to pay taxes all at once, but you can pay a loan in a lot of small payments. A loan costs more, because you have to pay interest on it. But you gain time, and small payments are easier to make."

"Except," Pico said with anger in his voice, "a Mexican-American with more land than money does not get a bank loan often in California. An old friend and neighbor, Emiliano Paz, gave us the mortgage to pay our taxes. Now we cannot pay the mortgage, and that is why we come to you, Jupiter."

"To me?"

"While I live, we will sell no more Alvaro land," Pico said fiercely. "But over many generations the Alvaros gathered much furniture, art, books, clothing, tools, and such. It is painful to part with our history, but we must make our payments, and it is time to sell what we can. I have heard that your uncle Titus will buy such things for a fair price."

"Will he!" Pete exclaimed. "And the older, the better."

"I think," Jupiter said, "that Uncle Titus will be delighted. Come on!"

Jupiter, an orphan, lived on the outskirts of Rocky Beach with his uncle Titus and aunt Mathilda. Across the street from their small house was the family business, The Jones Salvage Yard. This super-junkyard was famous up and down the entire coast of southern California. It held not only the usual secondhand goods—old pipes and beams, cheap furniture, used appliances—but also many wonderful treasures that Uncle Titus had collected—carved wood paneling, old marble bathroom fixtures, wrought-iron grillwork.

Uncle Titus left the day-to-day running of the business to Aunt Mathilda. He was more interested in scouting for items to sell in the yard. Estate sales, garage sales, fire sales—he attended them all, and he liked nothing better than a chance to buy an old family's possessions. As Jupe and Pete had predicted, he jumped at the Alvaros' offer.

"What are we waiting for?" he said, his eyes gleaming.

Minutes later, the salvage-yard truck was heading north, away from the Pacific Ocean and toward the foothills of the coastal mountains and the Alvaro ranch. Hans, one of Uncle Titus's two big Bavarian helpers, was at the wheel, with Titus and Diego beside him. Jupiter, Pete, Bob, and Pico rode in the back of the open pickup truck. The November afternoon was still sunny, but dark clouds were building over the mountains.

"Do you think those clouds will finally bring some rain?" asked Bob. No rain had fallen since the previous May, but the winter rains could start anytime.

Pico shrugged. "Perhaps. These are not the first clouds

we have seen this fall. We could use the rain soon. The Alvaro rancho is lucky to have a reservoir, but it must be filled every year. Now the water level is very low."

Pico looked out at the dry brown countryside dotted with dusty green live oaks.

"Once," he said, "all this was Alvaro land. Up and down the coast, and far over the mountains. Over twenty thousand acres."

"The Alvaro Hacienda." Bob nodded. "We learned about it in school. A land grant from the King of Spain."

"Yes," Pico said. "Our family has been in the New World a long time. Juan Cabrillo, the first European to find California, claimed it for Spain in 1542. But Carlos Alvaro was in the Americas even before that! He was a soldier with the conquistador Hernando Cortés when he defeated the Aztec Empire and conquered southern Mexico in 1521."

"Gosh, that was a hundred years before the Pilgrims landed at Plymouth Rock!" exclaimed Pete.

"When did the Alvaros come to California?" asked Jupiter.

"Much later," answered Pico. "The Spanish did not settle California until more than two hundred years after Cabrillo's discovery. California was very far from the capital of New Spain in Mexico City, and fierce Indians and harsh country lay in the way. At first the Spanish could reach California only by sea."

"They even thought California was an island, didn't they?" said Jupe.

Pico nodded. "For a while. Then, in 1769, Captain Gaspar de Portolá led an expedition north and reached San Diego by land. My ancestor Lieutenant Rodrigo Alvaro was with him. Portolá went on to discover San

Francisco Bay, and finally built a settlement in Monterey in 1770. On the way north, my ancestor Rodrigo saw the area that is now Rocky Beach, and he later decided to settle here. He applied to the provincial governor of California for land and was given a grant in 1784."

"I thought the King of Spain gave him the land," said Pete.

Pico nodded. "In a sense, he did. All the land of New Spain officially belonged to the king. But the governors of Mexico and California could make land grants on his behalf. Rodrigo received five square leagues—more than twenty-two thousand acres. Now we have only one hundred acres left."

"What happened?" asked Bob.

"Eh?'" Pico said, looking out of the truck at the land. "In a way, Pete, perhaps justice. We Spanish took the land from the Indians, and others took it from us. Over the years there were many Alvaro children, and the land was divided many times. Some was sold, some given away, some stolen by the tricks of enemies and colonial officials. It seemed a small matter, there was so much land.

"After California became part of the United States in 1848, there were ownership disputes and losses for taxes. Slowly our rancho became too small to be profitable. But our family has always been proud of its Spanish-Mexican heritage—I am named for the last Mexican governor of California, Pio Pico, and a statue of the great Cortés still stands on our land—and the Alvaros refused to give up being rancheros. When they couldn't make the rancho pay, they sold off the land to live."

"Now Mr. Norris wants the rest!" Pete exclaimed.

"He will not get it," Pico declared firmly. "It is poor land, and there is not enough for cattle now, but we raise

some horses, grow avocado trees, and work a small vegetable farm. My father and uncle worked often in town to
support the rancho. Now that they are dead, Diego and
I will do as they did if we must."

The county road that the salvage-yard truck was on had
been climbing north through hilly land. Now it reached a
large, open area that was fairly flat. The road curved
slowly left, to the west. In the middle of the curve, a dirt
road meandered off to the right.

Pico pointed up the dirt road. "That leads through the
Norris Ranch."

The Investigators could see the Norris ranch buildings
in the distance, but they couldn't make out the vehicles
by them. They wondered if Skinny and Cody had returned.

As the county road completed its turn to the west, it
crossed a small stone bridge over a dry creek bed.

"This is Santa Inez Creek—the boundary of our land,"
said Pico. "It will not have water in it until the rains come.
Our dam on the creek is about a mile north of here—at
the head of these ridges."

The ridges Pico referred to began just past the creek,
rising to the right of the county road. They were a series
of small, steep, narrow hills that reached down like long
fingers from the mountains to the north.

As the truck passed the last ridge, Pico pointed to its
top. There, black against the sky, was a large statue of a
man on a rearing horse. The man had one arm raised, as
if beckoning an unseen army to follow him.

"The conquistador Cortés," said Pico proudly. "The
symbol of the Alvaros. Indians made the statue almost
two hundred years ago. Cortés is the Alvaro hero."

Past the last ridge, the land flattened out again and the
road crossed another bridge over a deep, dry gully.

"Another dry creek?" asked Pete.

"I wish it were," said Pico. "But it is only an arroyo. Rain water collects in it after a big storm, but it has no source of water in the mountains, as Santa Inez Creek does."

Now the salvage-yard truck turned right, onto a dirt road with avocado trees growing alongside. Soon it turned right again, into a broad, bare yard.

"Welcome to Hacienda Alvaro," said Pico.

As the Investigators piled out into the dust, they saw a long, low adobe hacienda with whitewashed walls, deep-set windows, and a sloping, red-tiled roof. Held up by dark brown posts and beams, the roof overhung a ground-level brick veranda that ran along the front of the house. To the left was a one-story adobe horse barn. The ground in front of it had been fenced in to form a corral. Twisted oaks grew around the corral and barn and over the hacienda. Everything looked worn and bleak under the cloudy November sky.

A short distance behind the hacienda was the dry arroyo that the truck had crossed on the main road, and beyond that the ridges loomed up. Jupiter pointed out the statue of Cortés to his uncle.

"Is it for sale?" Uncle Titus asked Pico quickly.

"No," Pico said, "but there are many other things in the barn."

Hans backed the truck up to the corral while the others hurried across the dusty ground and into the barn. The light was dim inside, and Pico tossed his hat onto a wooden peg so he could see better to point out the family treasures. Uncle Titus and the Investigators gaped at what they saw.

Half the long building held horse stalls and ordinary

farming equipment. But the other half was a storehouse. Piled from floor to ceiling were tables, chairs, trunks, bureaus, chests, oil lamps, tools, draperies, bowls, pitchers, tubs, and even an old two-wheeled carriage! Uncle Titus was speechless at the sight of such fabulous treasure.

"The Alvaros had many houses," Pico explained. "Now there is only the hacienda, but the furnishings of all the other houses are here."

"I'll buy them all right now!" Uncle Titus exclaimed.

"Look!" Bob said. "Old armor! A helmet, and a breastplate!"

"Swords, and a saddle with silver trim!" Pete added.

The visitors started eagerly rummaging through the storehouse. But Uncle Titus had barely begun to take stock of the objects when a voice shouted outside. He raised his head. Two voices shouted now.

Everyone stopped what he was doing and listened. The voices came again—more clearly this time.

"Fire! Fire!"

*Fire!* Pell-mell, everyone rushed toward the door.

# 3

# Fire!

As they ran from the barn, the Investigators could faintly
smell smoke in the air. Two men stood in the yard waving
and shouting.

"Pico! Diego! There!"

"Beyond the dam!"

Pico went pale. From the corral, everyone could see a
column of smoke rising into the cloudy sky from the dry
brown mountains to the north. It signaled the most deadly
danger of all in the thick mesquite and chaparral of the
canyons of southern California—a brush fire!

"We called the firemen and the forest station!" one of
the two men shouted. "Hurry, get shovels and axes!"

"We must ride out!" the other yelled. "Get your horses!"

"Use our truck!" Jupiter cried.

"Yes!" Pico agreed. "Shovels and axes are in the barn!"

Big Hans ran to start the truck while everyone else
grabbed tools from the barn. Diego and Uncle Titus
jumped into the cab with Hans. The others swarmed into
the open back, where they stood holding tightly to the
sides as the truck took off. Breathlessly, Pico introduced
the two men who had given the alarm.

"Our friends Leo Guerra and Porfirio Huerta. For many
generations their families worked for Hacienda Alvaro.
Now Leo and Porfirio have small houses up the road and
work in town. But they still help us on our rancho."

The two short, black-haired men greeted the boys politely, then looked anxiously ahead over the truck cab as Hans turned toward the mountains along the narrow dirt road through the Alvaro ranch. Their wind-creased, leathery faces were worried, and they rubbed their hands nervously on their old, patched jeans.

As the truck drove north the smoke thickened, almost blotting out the cloudy sunlight. The Investigators were dimly aware of passing a large vegetable garden with irrigation ditches, then a group of horses racing southward in a field. At first the dirt road ran parallel to the dry arroyo and the ridges. Then, as it reached the mountains ahead, it forked. The fire was clearly up the right fork. Hans hurled the truck along the rutted road toward the spreading smoke. The road angled in toward the dry arroyo, which soon came to an abrupt end in the base of a high, rocky ridge. Just beyond this point the ridge itself ended, and then the truck was passing an old stone dam on the right. Below the dam, the dry bed of Santa Inez Creek curved away to the southeast along the far side of the ridge. Behind the dam was the reservoir—no more than a narrow pond at the foot of a low mountain. As the truck raced around the pond, flames became visible leaping up through the smoke ahead.

"Stop here!" Pico yelled from the back of the truck.

The truck screeched to a halt less than a hundred yards from the advancing fire, and everyone piled out.

"Spread out as wide as you can!" Pico ordered. "Try to dig a break in the brush. Throw dirt toward the flames. Maybe we can force the fire toward the pond! Hurry!"

The fire burned in a wide semicircle on both sides of the creek above the dam pond. It was an eerie line of advancing black, with smoke towering and spreading above and flames leaping like half-hidden devils below. One instant there would be live gray-green brush, and the next there was only blackened ash.

"At least there's not much wind!" Pete yelled. "Dig, guys!"

They spread out in front of the slowly advancing fire on the left side of the creek, and began to cut down small trees, clear brush, dig a shallow trench, and throw the dirt toward the fire.

"Look!" Bob pointed across the creek. "It's Skinny and that manager, Cody!"

Across the creek Skinny, the ranch manager Cody, and a lot of other men poured out of the Norris ranch wagon and two other trucks. With axes and shovels they began to fight the fire on that side. Jupiter saw that even Mr. Norris was there, waving his arms and bawling orders.

The two groups, barely visible to each other through the smoke and flames, battled the fire alone for what seemed like hours. But judging by the height of the sun, which showed occasionally through the smoke and darkening clouds, the Investigators knew it was less than half an hour before the whole fire-fighting power of the county was there.

The men of the forest service moved in with chemical tanks and bulldozers. Sheriff's deputies joined the Alvaro and Norris forces. Fire trucks from all the departments of Rocky Beach and the county roared through the dry brush on every side. Pumper trucks backed up to the pond and creek, and soon powerful streams of water hit the advancing fire.

The civilian trucks on both sides of the creek were commandeered to bring up waiting volunteers. The Investigators watched Hans drive off in the salvage-yard truck. Across the creek, the Norris trucks and ranch wagon raced south toward the county road.

Helicopters and old World War II bombers swooped in low over the flames and smoke, dropping tanks of water and red fire-retardant chemicals. Some of the planes made their runs over parts of the fire out of sight over the mountain. Others swept in directly over the fire fighters, drenching them.

For another hour the battle seemed hopeless. The fire burned steadily on and on. The fire fighters had to keep retreating to avoid being overcome by smoke. But the absence of wind, and the prompt action of everyone on the Alvaro and Norris ranches, slowly began to tell. The fire finally seemed to hesitate. Still burning furiously, covering the entire sky and land with heavy smoke, the fire seemed to mark time, to march in place like a stalled army.

Stalled, but not stopped! And the trucks continued to drive back and forth between the fire and the distant county road to bring up more volunteers.

"Keep working!" the fire captains shouted grimly. "It can still break loose any second!"

Ten minutes later Jupiter straightened up wearily to wipe his sweating face. He felt something hit his cheek and suddenly shouted:

"Rain! Pico! Uncle Titus! It's raining!"

Big drops of rain fell slowly all around. The long line of fire fighters paused and stared upward. Then the sky seemed to open, and a deluge engulfed their smoke-blackened faces. A ragged cheer went up and down the line as the fire hissed and steamed.

"Rain!" Bob exulted, his soot-streaked face turned up, as the torrential downpour went on. Thunder boomed every once in a while.

Smoke drifted everywhere, and pockets of flame continued to lick at the charred slopes, but the danger was over. The volunteers began to pack up and move out, leaving the firemen and forest service to mop up.

Blackened, wet and weary, the Alvaro forces gathered on the dirt road by the dam pond. Hans had not yet returned from his latest mission in the salvage-yard truck. The downpour began to slacken into a steady drizzle, and the late afternoon sky brightened a little.

"Come," Pico said. "We will walk back. It is less than a mile, and we will be warmer if we keep moving.

Tired, wet, but happy, the Investigators trooped down the road with the others. The narrow dirt road, muddy from the rain, was packed with trucks and volunteers all moving slowly south. Ahead loomed the high ridge that separated Santa Inez Creek from the dry arroyo.

Pico eyed the crowded, muddy road and led his group off it to the left.

"There is a faster and more pleasant way to return to the hacienda," he explained to the Investigators and Uncle Titus.

They skirted the dam and found themselves on a large, brush-covered mound at the base of the high ridge. It was this mound that blocked the arroyo on the west side of the ridge. A faint path led down to the creek bed, thirty feet below the dam. Before walking down it, everyone turned to look back. The whole countryside on both sides of the creek above the dam was a charred waste.

"Burned land will not hold water," Leo Guerra said grimly. "If the rain goes on, there will be floods."

Chastened, the group walked down the mound and along the bank of the now muddy creek bed. On the far bank was the dirt road that went through the Norris Ranch. It, too, was crowded with vehicles and fire fighters returning to the county road. The Investigators saw the Norris ranch wagon drive slowly past. Skinny was in the back with some other people. He saw the boys across the creek bed, but even he was too tired to react.

"Is that Norris land right over there?" Bob asked.

Pico nodded. "The creek is our boundary from the county road until just before the dam. Then the boundary goes northeast a short distance into the mountains. The dam and the creek above it are all on our land."

The high, rocky ridge on the group's right now dipped low. Beyond it the Investigators could see the whole series of ridges leading south. Pico turned away from the creek bed to follow a grassy trail through the small hills. Everyone strung out single file on the trail, enjoying the sight of unburned land. Low brush grew sparsely on the ridges, with brown rocks showing in between. Smoke still hung everywhere, but the rain had nearly stopped. The sun broke through the clouds once and then set.

Pete still had the energy to walk briskly, and Jupiter was too impatient a person to dawdle. The two boys soon found themselves in the lead. As they climbed the trail up the side of the last ridge, Pete and Jupiter were ten or twenty yards ahead of the others.

"Jupe!" Pete cried, pointing upward.

High on the ridge above them, through the drifting smoke, a man rode a great black horse! In the twilight, the boys stared up at the rearing horse, its massive hoofs pawing the smoke-filled air, its head . . .

"It—it—" Jupiter stammered, "—it's got no head!"

Rearing on the ridge, the great horse was headless!

"Run!" Pete yelled.

# 4

# The headless horse

The headless horse seemed to leap toward them through the smoke!

Bob and Diego ran up as Pete and Jupiter turned to flee. Farther back, Uncle Titus, Pico, Leo Guerra, and Porfirio Huerta hurried along the narrow trail through the ridges.

"It's got no head!" Pete yelled. "A ghost! Run!"

Bob stopped and stared up at the black horse and rider as the smoke thinned. His eyes widened.

"Jupe, Pete, it's just—" Bob began.

Diego laughed loudly. "It's the Cortés statue, fellows! The smoke made it look like it was moving!"

"It can't be Cortés!" Pete cried. "That statue of yours had a head!"

"Head?" Diego gaped. "Why, the horse's head *is* gone! Someone's broken our statue! Pico!"

"I see it," Pico said as he arrived with the others. "Let's take a look."

They swarmed up the smoky ridge to the wooden statue. The trunks of both the horse and rider had been crudely carved from single blocks of wood, with the legs, arms, sword, and saddle carved separately and attached. The horse was painted black, trimmed with the red and yellow of Castile. Under the high saddle, dabs of paint suggested an ornamental covering on the horse. The rider was painted black, too, except for a yellow beard, blue eyes, and red trim on his armor. All of the paint was faded.

"The statue used to be painted regularly," Diego explained, "but we haven't been able to take care of it right for a long time. I think the wood is getting rotten now."

In the grass beside the horse lay the broken-off head, its open mouth a faded red. Pico pointed to a heavy metal container on the ground nearby.

"There's what knocked the head off. It's a cylinder of chemicals for fire fighting. It must have fallen out of a plane or helicopter that passed over the statue."

Pete crouched down to study the head. The long wooden piece included most of the horse's neck, too. It had broken off cleanly. Both head and neck were hollow, as if the carver had wanted to lessen the weight of the wood before pegging it to the horse's body. Something projected slightly from the end of the hollow neck. Pete reached inside and pulled it out.

"What's this?" he asked.

"Let's see," Jupiter said, taking the object.

It was a long, thin cylinder of leather with dull metal fittings, hollow inside.

"It looks," Jupiter said slowly, "like a sword scabbard. You know, what a sword is carried in, the way a pistol is carried in a holster. Only—"

"Only it's too big inside," Bob said. "A sword would sure rattle around inside that."

"And there are no hooks to hang it from a belt," Jupe added.

"Let me see it," Pico said, taking the cylinder. He nodded. "Jupiter is partly right. It's not a sword scabbard, but it *is* a sword cover. It went over the scabbard to protect a valuable sword when it wasn't being worn. The cover looks quite old."

"Old? Valuable?" Diego was suddenly excited. "Maybe it was the cover of the Cortés Sword! Pete, look in the head—"

Pete was already searching inside the broken head. Then he stood and examined the whole statue. He shook his head.

"Nothing else inside the head and neck, and the bodies and legs are all solid."

"Foolishness, Diego," Pico snapped. "The Cortés Sword was lost long ago."

"A valuable sword?" Pete asked.

"Supposedly, Pete," Pico said, "although I sometimes wonder. It may have been just an ordinary sword that acquired a fabulous legend. It was in our family a very long time."

"Did it belong to Cortés himself?" Bob asked.

"So our family history says," Pico answered. "Our ancestor Don Carlos Alvaro, the first Alvaro in the New World, once saved Cortés's army from an ambush. In gratitude, Cortés presented Don Carlos with the sword. The story is that it was a special ceremonial sword given to Cortés by the King of Spain. It supposedly had a solid gold hilt and was all encrusted with jewels—the hilt, scabbard, even the blade. Rodrigo Alvaro brought the sword here when he settled on this land.

"What happened to it?" Jupiter asked.

"It vanished in 1846 at the start of the Mexican War, when Yankee soldiers came to Rocky Beach."

"You mean American soldiers stole it?" Pete exclaimed.

"Probably," Pico said. "All soldiers in enemy country have a habit of 'picking up' valuable items. The army officials later insisted that they had never even heard of the Cortés Sword, and maybe that was true. My great-great-grandfather, Don Sebastián Alvaro, was shot by the Americans attempting to escape from arrest. He fell into the ocean and was never found. The Yankee commander of the Rocky Beach garrison thought that the sword fell into the sea with him. In any case, it vanished. Perhaps it never was so fabulous. Just an ordinary old sword that my great-great-grandfather had with him when he escaped."

"But," Jupiter said thoughtfully, "no one really knows what happened to the sword, and someone must have put that old sword cover inside the statue's mouth, and—"

"Pico! The hacienda!"

Diego was standing at the edge of the ridge on the far side. Everyone ran to join him, and stared across the fields in horror. The hacienda was on fire!

"The barn's burning, too!" Uncle Titus cried.

"Hurry!" Pico shouted.

They raced down the slope and across the fields to the flames leaping into the evening sky. The smoke of the burning buildings mixed with the smoke still drifting from the last of the brush fire. A fire truck was parked in the dusty hacienda yard, and grimy fire fighters were trying to get close to the house with a hose. But even as the Alvaros and their friends reached the yard, the roofs of both the house and barn collapsed with a crash. There was nothing left now but burning ruins!

"Hopeless," a fire captain said to Pico. "Sorry, Alvaro. Sparks must have jumped over from the brush fire."

"How could that happen?" demanded Pete. "There was hardly any wind!"

"Hardly any at ground level," said the fire captain. "But there's often a good breeze just a little way above

the ground. Hot air rises from a fire, carrying sparks with it, and the upper-level winds can catch the sparks and carry them quite a distance. I've seen it happen before. It wouldn't have taken much to set fire to the dry old roof timbers in these buildings. And once the fire reached under the roof tiles, the rain couldn't put it out. If we'd seen the blaze sooner we might have saved something, but with all the smoke . . ."

The captain trailed off as two walls of the old hacienda fell in. The flames on the house died rapidly, with nothing left to burn. Pico and Diego stood in silence. The boys and Uncle Titus watched in dismay, unable to think of anything to say.

"The things in the barn!" Pete cried suddenly.

Uncle Titus, Bob, and Jupiter turned to look at the barn. It, too, was a smoldering ruin. Several walls still stood, but everything inside had burned. Everything that Uncle Titus had been going to buy from the Alvaros!

"Everything is lost," Pico said. "And we haven't any insurance. It is all over now."

"We can rebuild the hacienda!" Diego said fiercely.

"Yes," Pico said, "but how can we pay our mortgage? How can we keep the land to build on again?"

"Uncle Titus?" Jupiter said. "We agreed to buy those things in the barn, so they were as good as ours. I think we must pay for them."

Uncle Titus hesitated, then nodded. "Yes, I think you're right, Jupiter. A deal is a deal. Pico—"

Pico shook his head. "No, my friends, we cannot take such charity. I thank you for the generous thought, but we must keep our pride and honor if nothing else. No, we will sell our land to Mr. Norris, pay our debt to our neighbor, and find a home and work to do in town. Or perhaps it is time to return to Mexico."

"But you're Americans!" Bob protested. "The Alvaros have been here longer than anyone else!"

"Perhaps," Jupiter said slowly, "you can find the money you need somewhere else."

Pico smiled sadly. "There is no way, Jupiter."

"Maybe there is," the stocky leader of the Investigators said. "A long shot, but . . . Do you have to make those mortgage payments right away? And is there somewhere you can live for a while?"

"We can live with Señor Paz, our neighbor!" Diego said.

Pico nodded, "Yes, and I think we can wait a few weeks to pay him, Jupiter, but what—?"

"I've been thinking about that Cortés Sword," Jupiter explained. "If it *was* stolen during the Mexican War, it should have turned up *somewhere* in more than a hundred years. I'm sure soldiers would have sold it for cash at once. The fact that it never has shown up makes me wonder if it was really stolen at all. Maybe it was hidden just like that sword cover we found!"

Diego said eagerly, "Pico! I'll bet he's right! We—"

"Craziness!" Pico exploded. "There could be a hundred reasons why the sword has never been seen again! It could have fallen into the sea with Don Sebastián, or simply been accidentally destroyed. Perhaps soldiers sold it to someone whose family has quietly kept it all these years. It could be in China for all we know. You are jumping to conclusions because of that sword cover, but the cover could belong to any number of swords. No, finding the Cortés Sword is a childish fantasy, and we won't save our ranch with fantasies."

"That's all possible," Jupiter admitted, "but the sword

cover didn't get into the statue by accident. With enemy soldiers in town. Don Sebastián would have had good reason to hide a valuable sword. I think you should at least look for it, and we can help. Pete, Bob, and I have experience finding things."

"They're detectives, Pico," Diego said. "Show him, fellows."

Bob handed Pico their business card. It read:

THE THREE INVESTIGATORS
"We Investigate Anything"
? ? ?

First Investigator ................... Jupiter Jones
Second Investigator .............. Peter Crenshaw
Records and Research .............. Bob Andrews

When Pico looked skeptical, Jupiter handed him a second card. This one said:

*This certifies that the bearer is a Volunteer Junior Assistant Deputy cooperating with the police force of Rocky Beach. Any assistance given him will be appreciated.*

*(Signed) Samuel Reynolds*
*Chief of Police*

"I see you are detectives," Pico said, "but it is still a foolish idea. Who could find a sword lost for more than a hundred years?"

"Let them try, Pico!" Diego urged.

"It can't hurt," Uncle Titus added.

Pico looked at the ruins of his fine old hacienda and sighed. "Very well, they can try. I will help all I can, but you will forgive me if I am not optimistic. For instance, where will they begin, eh? How? With what? Where?"

"We'll think of something," Jupiter said lamely.

Soon after, Hans arrived with the truck. The Alvaros went with Guerra and Huerta to their neighbor Emiliano Paz, and the Investigators rode back to town. In the back of the truck, Pete asked:

"Jupe? Where *do* we start?"

"Why," Jupiter said with a grin, "the answer's in your hand."

"It is?" Pete looked down. He was holding the old sword cover.

"I didn't want to raise false hopes," Jupiter explained eagerly, "but I noticed something. There are small symbols on the metal fittings of the cover. We'll call Mr. Hitchcock, and maybe he can send us to someone who can identify those markings."

The stout leader's eyes gleamed. "I've got a hunch what they are already, and if I'm right, we'll be on our way to finding the Cortés Sword!"

# 5

# The search begins

"Fantastic!" Professor Marcus Moriarty cried, his eyes alight. "There can be no doubt, young man—those markings show the royal coat of arms of Castile!"

It was Friday afternoon, and the Three Investigators were sitting in the study of Professor Moriarty in Hollywood. Jupiter had called Alfred Hitchcock that morning, and the famous motion-picture director had named his friend Marcus Moriarty as the number-one expert on Spanish and Mexican history in Los Angeles. Mr. Hitchcock had agreed to call the professor and arrange an appointment. The moment school ended that day, the Investigators persuaded Hans to drive them to the professor's house.

"This sword cover undoubtedly belonged to the King of Spain in the early sixteenth century," the professor went on. "Where did you find it?"

Jupiter told him about the statue. "Is the cover old enough to have been the cover for the Cortés Sword of the Alvaros?"

"The Cortés Sword?" The professor's eyebrows rose. "Why, yes, the cover is from the same period as the sword. But, of course, the Cortés Sword was lost with Don Sebastián Alvaro back in 1846. Unless . . . don't tell me you've found the sword, too!"

"No, sir," Bob said.

"Not yet, anyway!" Pete beamed.

"Professor," Jupiter said, "where can we find out exactly what did happen to Don Sebastián Alvaro back in 1846? And where are reports of other events in those days?"

"The Rocky Beach Historical Society has all the Alvaro family papers, I believe," the professor said. "It also has copies of certain United States Army documents from the Mexican War years—those relating to this area. And, of course, the Historical Society would be the place to go for the most complete archives of local history from the earliest days."

The boys thanked him and got ready to leave.

"You'll find 1846 an interesting year to study," remarked the professor. "The Mexican War was a rather strange episode in Californian—and American—history."

"How's that?" asked Bob.

"The United States Government declared war on Mexico in May 1846 in what many people believe was merely an effort to take over Mexican territory, including California. Many Californians had become unhappy under Mexican rule—mostly Yankees who had settled here, but even some of the old Spanish rancheros. When U.S. naval ships seized the key California ports at the start of the war, there was virtually no resistance. Soldiers were then stationed along the coast—many of them were volunteers from one of John C. Frémont's American exploratory expeditions. Frémont happened to be in California at the time, and his group was acting like invaders even before war was declared."

"Yes, we learned about Major Frémont in school," said Bob.

"Well, as I said, there'd been no resistance at the ports, and everything seemed quiet. Of course, many of the rancheros weren't happy with the situation, but they gave no organized opposition. Then the Yankee commander that Frémont left in charge of Los Angeles proceeded to act with great misjudgment, arresting the local rancheros and humiliating them needlessly. The populace was soon up in arms. I suspect that Don Sebastián Alvaro was a victim of that commander's unfortunate policies. If Don Sebastián had lived, I'm sure he would have joined the fighting that broke out. The Alvaro family were Mexican loyalists; I believe Don Sebastián's son fought with the Mexican Army against the American invasion force in Mexico itself.

"In any event, the fighting in California lasted only a matter of months. California was soon securely held by the Americans, and Mexico formally ceded it to the United States at the end of the war, in 1848."

"Gosh," Pete said, "that must have been an exciting time here. Just think—a real war in our own backyard!"

Professor Moriarty gave Pete a severe look. "War may be exciting, perhaps, but it is never pleasant to live through. Be grateful you live in quieter times."

Pete looked abashed, and the professor softened his tone. "I suspect you boys find plenty of excitement anyway. Do I gather correctly that you have reason to think the Cortés Sword may still be in Rocky Beach, and that you are searching for it?"

"Well, it's just a wild hunch, sir," Jupiter said.

"I see," the professor said. His eyes glinted. "Since the sword hasn't been seen for so long, I've always thought that it was probably only a legend. Certainly an exaggerated tale, in any event. Still, I'd be most interested in anything you find, eh?"

"We'll be glad to let you know, sir," Jupiter said, and thanked the professor again for his help.

Outside, a slow rain had started. Hans had gone on some business for Uncle Titus and hadn't yet returned, so the boys had to wait. They stood under a tree, where they could keep dry.

"Professor Moriarty was pretty excited about that sword," Pete said. "I guess a lot of people would be."

"Yes," Jupiter said, frowning. "I think, fellows, that we had better not mention the Cortés Sword if we can help it. I'm afraid we'd start all kinds of people looking everywhere. Professor Moriarty's identification of the sword cover just about guarantees that it belongs to the Cortés Sword, so the chances of finding the sword in the Rocky Beach area are quite real."

"Are we going to the Historical Society now?" Bob asked.

"That, I think, is our next step, yes," Jupiter replied.

"What are we looking for, Jupe?" Pete asked.

"I don't know exactly," the stout leader admitted, "but if my hunch is right, we need something to show that events in 1846 didn't happen the way people think they did."

The rain grew heavier just as Hans arrived, and all three boys crowded into the truck cab beside the big Bavarian. When they reached Rocky Beach, Hans dropped them at the Historical Society and drove off on another errand. The boys hurried inside through the rain.

The quiet rooms, lined with books, files, and displays, were deserted except for the assistant historian. He knew the boys and their reputation well, and greeted them with a teasing smile.

"Well, what are you young Sherlocks investigating now?" he asked. "Has someone lost a pet cat, or are you onto something bigger?"

"Only as big as the Cor—" Pete began boastfully.

Jupiter stepped on Pete's foot, making him yelp in pain.

"Sorry," Jupiter said blandly, and smiled at the historian. "We're not on a case—just helping Bob with a research project on the Alvaro family for school."

"Well, we have an Alvaro file," the historian said.

"Might you have the U.S. Army reports about Don Sebastián Alvaro, too?" Jupiter added casually.

The historian got both files. Each was a large cardboard box filled with papers. The boys looked at them in dismay.

"This army file is just the records of 1846," the historian said, grinning. "They loved to write reports in those days."

The boys carried the heavy files to a quiet corner.

"I'll search the Alvaro file," Jupiter decided, "and you two can go through the army records. They're in English."

For the next two hours the boys pored over the papers in the files, searching for any references to Don Sebastián Alvaro or the Cortés Sword. The historian was busy cataloging a mound of new material, and he left the boys alone. No one else came into the quiet, book-lined rooms. The only sound was an occasional groan from Pete as he finished skimming yet another dull report.

At the end of the two hours, the Investigators had gone through both files completely and were ready to display their findings. Bob and Pete had three documents, modern copies of original U.S. Army papers from 1846, and Jupiter had a single yellowing letter.

"It's a letter that Don Sebastián wrote to his son," Jupiter explained. "It's all I could find that seems important. Don Sebastián wrote it when he was being held under

arrest in a house in Rocky Beach. His son was an officer in
the Mexican Army down in Mexico City."

"What does it say, Jupe?" Pete asked.

"Well, it's in old-fashioned Spanish and hard for me to
read," Jupiter admitted unhappily. "All it seems to say is
that the American soldiers arrested Don Sebastián, and
that he was being held prisoner in a house near the ocean.
There's something about visitors, and about everything
else being okay, and that he'd see his son in victory over
the invaders. That could be a hint about an escape, but I
can't be sure. The letter is dated September 13, 1846, and
there's nothing in it about a sword."

"Gosh, Jupe, remember he was under arrest," Pete
pointed out. "Maybe he used a code or something."

"Yes, that makes sense," Jupiter agreed. "We'd better
have Pico translate the letter word for word, and then—"

"Maybe it doesn't matter, fellows," Bob said. He held
up an army document. "This is a letter the U.S. Army
wrote to Don Sebastián's son José when José came home
after the war. It says that the U.S. Government regrets the
tragic death of Don Sebastián while attempting to escape
on September 15, 1846. It claims the soldiers had no
choice because Don Sebastián was armed and tried to re-
sist. He fell into the ocean when he was shot. The shooting
was reported by a Sergeant James Brewster, and corrobo-
rated by Corporal William McPhee and Private S. Crane.
They were the soldiers on duty in the house where Don
Sebastián was held."

"We knew all about that," Pete declared. "Pico told us."

Jupiter was puzzled. "That letter doesn't confirm all of
Pico's story. What about—"

"The original report of Sergeant Brewster is attached
to the letter," Bob said gloomily. "It gives the same facts

as the letter, except that it also says what Don Sebastián was armed with—a sword!"

Pete and Jupiter looked at Bob in dismay.

"The sergeant figured the sword was smuggled to Don Sebastián by some visitor," Bob went on. "So I guess Don Sebastián did fall into the ocean with a sword."

Jupiter stared out a window at the heavy rain, thinking hard. At last he asked, "What did you find, Pete?"

"Not much for around the same time," Pete answered, dejected. "Just a letter to a commanding officer on September 23 asking for details of the Mexican attack on the Los Angeles garrison early that morning, and naming some men absent without leave since September 16 and declaring them deserters. Nothing about Don Sebastián or any sword, so—"

Jupiter sat up straight. "What soldiers, Pete?"

Pete read the document. "Sergeant Brewster, Corporal McPhee, and Private—"

"Crane!" Bob cried.

Across the room, the assistant historian looked up in annoyance. The boys didn't even notice.

"Brewster, McPhee, and Crane!" said Jupe with satisfaction. "Missing after September 16, 1846!"

"Yeah, but—" Pete's eyes widened. "Wow! Those are the same three guys who shot Don Sebastián!"

"Who *claimed* they shot Don Sebastián," Jupiter pointed out.

"You think they were lying, Jupe?" Bob asked.

"I think," Jupiter said grimly, "that it's a very suspicious coincidence that the men who reported shooting Don Sebastián deserted the very next day and never came back."

"Does that mean they stole his sword?" Pete asked.

"Perhaps. But then who hid that sword cover in the

statue, and why? It's all very strange. We'd better talk to Pico."

"It's late, Jupe," Pete said. "I've got to get home for dinner."

"So do I," Bob added.

"Then we'll bike out to see Pico first thing tomorrow."

The Investigators made copies of the four documents on the Historical Society's duplicating machine. Then they thanked the historian for his help, and left. The rain was still falling steadily. They ran all the way to the salvage yard, where Bob and Pete had left their bikes, and got soaked for the second time in twenty-four hours.

A red sports car was parked just outside the salvage-yard entrance.

"All wet as usual," Skinny Norris called from the car.

"Not behind the ears like you," Pete retorted.

Skinny flushed. "I came to do you all a favor, and tell you to stay away from those Alvaros."

"Is that a threat?" Jupiter asked.

"Your father won't get their ranch!" Pete said hotly.

"What'll you three do to stop him?" Skinny sneered.

"We're going to find—" Pete began.

Jupiter kicked him. "We'll think of something, Skinny."

"Think fast." Skinny laughed nastily. "We'll have that ranch inside a week, so there! And those Alvaros are going to be in big trouble soon, so you better stay away, and just keep your big noses out of my dad's business!"

Skinny roared off with a squeal of tires. Standing in the rain, the boys looked after him uneasily. Skinny had sounded awfully confident.

# 6

# Bad news

Jupiter got up early Saturday morning, even though the rain was still coming down steadily. But he soon discovered that the planned visit to the Alvaros would have to be delayed. Both Bob and Pete had some chores to do at home first. Jupiter then made a bad mistake. Because of the rain, he remained in the house. Aunt Mathilda pounced on him and put him to work.

"Can't have you moping around because of a little rain!" Aunt Mathilda boomed heartily.

Groaning, and filing a mental note to never be caught again in the house on a Saturday even if there was a typhoon outside, Jupiter spent the morning sorting junk in the roofed-over section of the salvage yard. Let off for lunch, the stout leader of The Three Investigators ate quickly and slipped away to the team's secret headquarters. Headquarters was in an old, damaged house trailer, long forgotten under mounds of junk in one corner of the salvage yard.

Soon after, Bob and Pete arrived at Headquarters, and the three boys hurried back outside to their bikes. Protected by slickers, they biked through light rain out along the county road. Jupe carried a road map in case they got lost in the foothills. They rode past the ruins of the Alvaro hacienda and found the small avocado farm of the neighbor Emiliano Paz without trouble.

The Paz house was an old frame building with a big barn and two small cottages behind. Diego was out chopping wood in the rain near one cottage when the boys rode up.

"Is Pico home?"

"He is in the cottage," Diego said. "You have found—?"

Jupiter led them all into the little cottage. There were only two rooms and a tiny kitchen. Pico had just started a fire in the living room fireplace. He stood up to greet the Investigators.

"All wet as usual," Skinny Norris called from the car.

Jupiter told Pico and Diego what Professor Moriarty had said about the sword cover.

"It's almost certainly the cover of the Cortés Sword," Jupe concluded.

"And Don Sebastián wasn't shot escaping at all!" Pete cried.

"At least," Bob corrected his eager friend, "there's a chance he wasn't."

Jupiter showed the two Alvaros the copies of the army's letter to José Alvaro, the original report by Sergeant Brewster about the death of Don Sebastián, and the report of the desertion of Sergeant Brewster, Corporal McPhee, and Private Crane.

"So?" Pico said. "How do these documents change anything? We are told that Don Sebastián was shot—something we have no reason to doubt. And the sergeant's report implies that Don Sebastián had his sword with him when he fell into the sea. That's just what the Yankee commander told my family at the time."

"Don't you find it suspicious," Jupiter asked, "that the men who reported the escape and shooting of your great-great-grandfather all deserted from the army the next day?

One man deserting could be a coincidence, even two men, but all three?"

"All right," Pico said. "Then it is as I always thought. The sword wasn't lost in the sea. The three men stole it before shooting Don Sebastián. Then they filed their report, deserted, and vanished with the sword."

"That's possible," Jupiter agreed. "But what about the cover? Who hid it in the statue? It almost had to be Don Sebastián, and the only reason would have been to hide the sword from the Americans. Except for some reason he separated the sword and scabbard from the cover."

"The cover might have been hidden by whoever smuggled the sword in to Don Sebastián," Pico pointed out.

"That's another fishy part of the story," Jupe said. "Why smuggle a valuable sword practically into the hands of the enemy? If Don Sebastián needed a weapon, why not take him a gun? He couldn't very well fight with a jewel-covered ceremonial sword."

Pico shrugged. "We don't know for sure there were jewels."

"Well, here's what I think might have happened back then," said Jupiter. "The Americans really arrested Don Sebastián to try to get the Cortés Sword. Yes, Bob, I know what Professor Moriarty said," Jupe interrupted his account as he saw Bob about to object, "but Frémont's soldiers could have been greedy, as well as eager to control local leaders. The men in Rocky Beach could easily have heard about Don Sebastián's fabulous sword. Now, say Don Sebastián had hidden the sword in the statue. When he escaped from arrest, Sergeant Brewster and his two confederates went after him. They decided to try to get the sword for themselves, so they cooked up the shooting story to hide what they were doing. Then they deserted and went looking for Don Sebastián and the sword. Don Sebastián was afraid they'd find the sword where it was, so he got it and rehid it. He left the cover in the statue—maybe to confuse them."

"And what happened to Don Sebastián?" Pico said.

"I don't know," Jupiter said lamely.

"You don't know very much, Jupiter," Pico said, shaking his head, "and all you've said is the wildest speculation. Even if you are partly right, and my great-great-grandfather did escape alive, where did he hide the sword, and how will you find it?"

"What about Don Sebastián's letter, Jupe?" Bob said.

Jupiter nodded quickly, and handed the copy of the letter to Pico.

"Would you translate it, Pico?" he asked, and motioned to Bob. "Write down the translation, Records."

"Records?" repeated Diego, "why do call him Records?"

"Because he's the Records and Research man of The Three Investigators," explained Jupiter," We sometimes call Pete 'Second' because he's the Second Investigator, And I'm First!"

Pico had been studying Don Sebastián's letter. "I know this letter," he said. "My grandfather often read it looking for a clue to the lost sword, but he never found one." He translated the letter aloud: " 'Condor Castle, September 13, 1846. My dear José, I hope you are well and doing your duty as a Mexican. The Yankees are in our poor town, and I have been arrested. They will not tell me why, but I suspect, eh? I am a prisoner in the Cabrillo house near the sea, and they will let no one visit me or even speak to me. The others of our family are well, and all else is safe. Soon, I know, we will meet in our victory!' "

Bob looked at what he had written in his notebook.

"That stuff about suspecting why he was arrested," he said. "You think he meant that the Americans wanted the sword, just as Jupe said?"

"And what about 'all else is safe!'" Pete exclaimed. "Maybe he was telling José the sword was safely hidden!"

"Let me see," Jupiter said, taking Bob's notebook. "Perhaps you're both right. I'm not sure. But I am sure now that Sergeant Brewster *was* lying in his report!"

"What makes you sure of that, Jupiter?" Pico asked.

"Sergeant Brewster stated in his report of the escape and shooting that Don Sebastián was armed with a sword, probably smuggled to him by a visitor! But Don Sebastián wasn't allowed any visitors, so he couldn't have been smuggled a sword! Brewster made that up to justify his story of the shooting, and to make people think that the sword was lost. I'm convinced the whole report was a lie to hide what he and his friends were up to!"

Pico studied the letter. "Yes, I see, but I still—"

Outside in the rain there was a loud thud, a crash, and then the sound of logs rolling together. Feet pounded away.

"You! Stop!" a voice cried out.

The Investigators and the Alvaros ran from the cottage. They were just in time to see a horse galloping away to the left beyond the barn. A small, white-haired old man stood in the yard.

"Someone was listening at your window, Pico!" the old man cried. "I was coming to speak with you, and saw him! When he heard me, he ran and fell over the stack of firewood. He went behind the barn. He had a horse there!"

"Did you see who it was?" Diego cried.

The old man shook his head. "My eyes are not what they once were, Diego. A man or boy, I could not tell."

"You are getting wet, Don Emiliano," Pico said, his voice and manner respectful to the old man. "Come inside, please."

Inside the cottage, Pico sat the old man near the fire, and introduced him to the boys. Emiliano Paz smiled at them.

"Was he out there very long, sir?" Jupiter asked.

"I do not know. Only now did I come from the house."

"Who do you think it was, First?" Bob asked. "Why would he be listening at the Alvaros' window?"

"I don't know," Jupiter said, "but I wonder if he heard us talking about the Cortés Sword?"

"Is that bad, Jupe?" Pete said.

"I suspect that Mr. Norris and his people wouldn't want us to find a valuable sword," Jupiter said grimly. "Last night, Skinny was pretty interested in what we might be doing."

"I do not think it matters, Jupiter," Pico said. "If all your speculations are true, they still tell us nothing about where the sword could be, or even if it still exists at all."

"I'm sure that Don Sebastián knew those three soldiers were after the sword, and that he hid it," Jupiter declared stubbornly. "And I'm sure he would have left a clue for his son. If not in that letter, then somewhere. But there should be some clue in the letter. He was a prisoner and in danger, and he must have thought it might be his only chance to tell José where to find the sword."

They all looked at the letter again. Pico and Diego re-read the original, and the Investigators studied the translation Bob had taken down.

"If there's a code, I sure don't see it," Pete said.

Pico shook his head. "It is a simple letter, Jupiter. I see nothing that could be a clue or a code in the Spanish."

"Except maybe those hints about everything being safe," Diego said.

"Jupe?" Bob said suddenly. "That heading at the top, above the date—Condor Castle. What is that? Do you know, Pico?"

"No," Pico said slowly, puzzled. "A place, I think. People in those days, and even today, often put where they are writing from at the top of a letter. A town, a hacienda, a house."

"But," Bob said, "Don Sebastián wrote the letter in a Cabrillo house."

"And his home was your hacienda," Jupiter added. "Was it ever called Condor Castle?"

"No," Pico said. "It was always Hacienda Alvaro."

"Then why did he write Condor Castle at the top?" Pete cried. "Unless it was some special place that José would know about! A clue!"

Jupiter pulled out his road map of the county. Everyone else peered over his shoulder as he studied it. Then Jupiter sighed and sat back.

"No Condor Castle," he said unhappily, and then looked up. "Wait! This is a modern map! In 1846 the map would—"

"I have an old map," Emiliano Paz said.

The old man left the cottage. The others waited for him impatiently. At last the old man came back with a yellowed old map. Dated 1844, it was half in Spanish and half in English. Both Pico and Jupiter read it carefully.

"Nothing," Pico said. "There is no Condor Castle."

"No," Jupiter had to agree.

Pico looked defeated and angry. "Foolishness, as I said! We will not save our ranch with a pipe dream! No, we must find a better—"

Emiliano Paz said sadly, "Perhaps you have no other way, Pico. I am sorry, but I came to speak to you of bad news. You are very far behind with your mortgage payments. It is much money for me, and soon I must pay my own debts. I lent to you all the money I had, and now with all you own burned with your hacienda, you cannot pay me. I must have the money, and Mr. Norris has offered to buy your mortgage. I have come to tell you that very soon I must sell to him."

Pete whispered, "That's what Skinny meant last night!"

"I thank you for coming to me, Don Emiliano," Pico said. "What must be, must be. You have your own family to consider."

"I am sorry. Will you honor me by staying here?"

"Of course, Don Emiliano," Pico said. "We are friends."

The old man nodded and walked slowly out of the cottage. His head was bent as he crossed the muddy yard in the rain. Pico looked after him for a moment, and then went outside, too. Soon the boys heard him chopping wood.

"It's all over," Diego said hopelessly.

"No, it isn't!" Jupiter insisted firmly. "We'll find the Cortés Sword, Diego!"

"We will!" Bob echoed.

"You bet we will!" Pete chimed in. "We'll . . . we'll . . . Gosh, Jupe, what will we do?"

"Tomorrow, we'll look for every old map we can find," the stout leader of the trio declared. "Condor Castle must be some secret clue, and we'll find it. We'll study every old map in Rocky Beach if we have to!"

"And I'll help!" Diego cried.

The four boys smiled at each other.

# 7

# The old map

The rain slowed to a drizzle Sunday morning. Diego borrowed a bike and a raincoat from the family of Emiliano Paz and rode into town. He met Jupiter in front of the Historical Society around noon.

"Bob's covering the library," Jupiter explained, "and Pete's dad got him special permission to look at the maps in the County Land Office."

"We'll find Condor Castle," Diego exclaimed. "I know it!"

They hurried into the Historical Society. People were already reading and studying at the tables of the hushed, book-lined rooms, and the assistant historian was busy. But as he directed the boys to the map room, he remarked:

"Someone else was in to look at the Alvaro papers. A tall, thin boy. He seemed to be concerned with what papers you had copied, Jupiter. Of course, I didn't tell him."

"Skinny!" Jupiter exclaimed when he and Diego were out of earshot. "He's really worried about what we're doing."

"Because he knows all the valuable things you've found on other cases," Diego said, "and he's afraid you'll find a treasure for us."

"I hope we do," Jupiter said, "but we don't have much time."

In the map room, the boys were alone. They found almost fifty maps from around 1846, some of the whole county, and some of just the Rocky Beach area. They didn't find Condor Castle.

"Here's a map of just the Alvaro ranch," Jupiter said.

"Look how big it was then," Diego said sadly.

"But still no Condor Castle!"

"And that's all the maps from Don Sebastián's time."

"All right," Jupiter said, refusing to give up, "we'll look at every map of Rocky Beach no matter how new!"

"Or old!" Diego said.

There weren't very many modern maps, and only a few from before the 1840s. Condor Castle appeared on none of them. There was nothing for Diego and Jupiter to do but give up and go back to Headquarters in the salvage yard.

"Maybe Bob or Pete will find something," Jupiter said hopefully.

He led Diego into Headquarters by the main entrance —a large pipe that went under a huge mound of junk and ended at a trap door in the floor of the hidden mobile home trailer.

"We call this Tunnel Two," the stocky leader of the Investigators explained as he and Diego crawled through the pipe. "We've got other entrances, too, but we use this one the most. The others are for emergencies."

"Gee!" Diego exclaimed as he emerged through the trap door into the hidden trailer. He stared around at the desk, telephone, typewriter, files, electronic equipment, darkroom, birdcages, plaster statues, and all the other tools and souvenirs the boys had collected in their work.

"This is great!"

"I believe we are very adequately equipped," Jupiter said a little pompously. We built or gathered all of it ourselves."

"No wonder you solve tough mysteries so easily!"

"Not always so easily," Jupiter said glumly. "Finding any clues to the Cortés Sword seems extremely difficult."

"Bob or Pete will find something," Diego assured him.

As they waited impatiently, Diego wandered around the secret headquarters examining everything. He couldn't see outside because the junk hiding the trailer was piled against its tiny windows. Jupiter sat frowning, his round face not unlike the gloomy bust of Alfred Hitchcock on the filing cabinet behind him. Then the trap door opened, and Bob came in.

"Nothing!" the Records and Research man said, and dropped into a chair looking as gloomy as Jupiter. "I looked at every book about the county that the library has."

When Pete finally emerged through the trap door, the others only had to look at his face.

"If Condor Castle means anything, fellows," the tall Second Investigator said, "I guess only Don Sebastián and José knew what."

"We're at a dead end, First," Bob concluded.

Diego was near tears. "Don't give up, fellows! We—"

Pete sat up alertly. "Shh! Listen!"

For a long moment there was only silence inside the hidden trailer. Then everyone heard it—a faint rattle of metal outside in the salvage yard. It came again, from a slightly different spot, and then there was a sound of tapping.

"Shhhh," Jupiter whispered, his finger on his lips.

The rattle came again—from still another spot.

Someone is out there moving and testing the junk," Bob said softly. "Someone who thinks we're in here!"

"Did anyone follow either of you?" Jupiter asked quietly.

"Not me," Bob whispered.

"I . . . I'm not sure," Pete said. "I was in a hurry, I didn't check."

"No one moves or speaks," Jupiter ordered.

The poking and tapping among the piles of junk that covered the trailer went on for some minutes. Then there was silence.

"Take a look, Bob," Jupiter whispered.

The Records and Research man stepped softly to the See-All, a homemade periscope that went up through the roof. From outside, it looked like a simple piece of old pipe sticking up at the top of a junk mound. Bob looked through the eyepiece.

"He's going away across the yard," Bob reported. "It's that ranch manager, Cody! He's still looking around. Now he's leaving the salvage yard. He's gone, fellows!"

Bob turned from the See-All. "He must have followed one of us to see what we're doing. Jupe, could he have been the eavesdropper at Emiliano Paz's place yesterday?"

"I suspect as much," Jupiter said thoughtfully. "Skinny and that Cody seem very interested in our actions. I wonder if they have any more reason than to help Mr. Norris get the Alvaro ranch?"

"Maybe they know something about the sword and want to find it for themselves!" Diego exclaimed.

"That is possible, Diego."

"If they know anything, it's more than we do," Pete said.

Jupiter nodded sadly. "I was certain we would find an old map that would tell us what and where Condor Castle was."

"Maybe we need an old Indian map, and an old Indian to read it for us." Pete laughed.

"Very funny, Second," Bob groaned. "Jokes won't help us—"

"Pete!" Jupiter cried. "I think you've got it!"

"Gosh, First, it wasn't that bad a joke. You don't have to—"

"No," Jupiter said, "I mean it! That could be the answer! Of course, I've been stupid!"

"What answer, First?" Pete said, confused.

"A *really* old map! If Don Sebastián had used a name everyone could find on a map in 1846, the Americans would have spotted it! He knew they would study the letter—so he used a name from a map so old and rare even in 1846 only he and José would recognize it! I never thought to ask the historian for *really* old maps—and they'd be too valuable just to leave out in the map room. Come on, fellows! Back to the Historical Society!"

They scrambled out through Tunnel Two, checking carefully at the end of the pipe to be sure that Cody, or anyone else, wasn't watching. Jupiter led the race to their bikes.

As the boys rode out of the salvage yard, a voice boomed across the street:

"JUPITER!"

Aunt Mathilda was standing on the stoop of the Jones house looking angry.

"Where have you been, you scamp! Have you forgotten your great-uncle Matthew's birthday party? We have to leave in fifteen minutes! Get over here and put on your good suit! You'll have to see your friends another time."

"Oh, no!" groaned Jupe. "I forgot! It's my great-uncle's eightieth birthday," he explained to his friends. "There's a family party for him clear on the other side of Los Angeles. I can't get out of going, and I'm sure we won't be back until very late. You'll have to carry on without me."

"*Jupiter!*" Aunt Mathilda's voice held an ominous warning note.

Jupe sadly waved good-bye to the other boys and went across the street.

"Now what?" asked Pete.

"To the Historical Society, of course," answered Bob, taking charge. And in a minute, the boys had forgotten all about Jupiter as their excitement over Condor Castle rose again.

When the assistant librarian heard the boys' latest request, he thought a moment. "A really early map of this area?" he said. "Yes, we do have one in our rare documents collection. One of the very first, from 1790. It's so delicate we rarely bring it out into the light and show it."

"Please, sir," Bob urged, "may we look at it?"

The historian hesitated, and then nodded. He led them to the back where he unlocked a door. They all went into a windowless room which had its temperature and humidity kept at a constant level. All the documents were in glass cases or on shelves behind glass doors. The historian checked his files, then unlocked a drawer and drew out a long, flat glass case. Inside the case was a crude old map drawn in brown lines on thick, yellowed paper.

"Just look at it through the glass, please," the historian said.

The boys bent over the ancient map of the Rocky Beach area.

"There," Diego pointed in awe. "In Spanish: Condor Castle!"

"It's there!" Bob exulted.

"Right on the Alvaro rancho, if that squiggly line is supposed to be Santa Inez Creek," Diego said.

"What are we waiting for?" Pete cried.

The boys thanked the astonished historian, and ran out to their bikes.

# 8

# Condor castle

The rain had stopped, but dark clouds still swept low over the mountains as the two Investigators and Diego rode along the dirt road of the Alvaro ranch. They were headed toward the old dam where they had battled the brush fire. As the road curved in alongside the dry arroyo and the ridge before the dam, Diego stopped.

"If I read the map right, Condor Castle is the rock peak at the end of this last ridge," the slim boy said. "Santa Inez Creek is just on the other side of it."

They left their bikes hidden in the brush beside the road, and pushed through the heavy chaparral to the edge of the deep arroyo. The dam was out of sight to their left, beyond the low, brush-covered mound that closed off the arroyo.

The boys looked across the arroyo and up at the top of the high ridge. At the left end of it, just before the ridge dropped sharply off to the low mound, the tall rock peak jutted up.

"That must be it!" Diego said again. "Right where the map showed it."

"What's it called now?" Pete asked as they scrambled down into the muddy arroyo and started up the ridge on the far side.

"Nothing, as far as I know," Diego said.

The high ridge sloped in two sections: the lower two-thirds was a gentle slope covered with big boulders and brush; and the upper one-third was steeper and almost all rock with no brush. The boys were puffing when they climbed the last third and stood on top of the giant rock that crowned the long ridge.

"Condor Castle," Bob said, awestruck.

From the great rock the whole countryside was visible except to the north, where the mountains towered. But before the mountains rose, the boys could see the dam and the creek beyond with the charred brush on both sides.

"The creek's swollen above the dam," Diego pointed out, "and the dam's already spilling a little. We'll have a real creek below if it keeps on raining."

Bob pointed down to the low mound at the base of the ridge. "Look how that mound separates the arroyo from the creek and the dam," he said. "If the mound weren't there, you'd have a second creek."

The boys turned around and studied the rest of the view. To the west, they could see the road and the deep arroyo that reached south to the ruins of the hacienda almost a mile away. Directly to the south, more ridges fanned out. Far beyond them, the boys could make out Rocky Beach itself and the ocean, dark in the gray day. To the east, on the other side of the high ridge, Santa Inez Creek curved to the southeast. A trickle of water showed in it now. Across the creek bed, the flat brushland spread out, and they could see the Norris ranch houses and corrals a mile or so away. The road through the Norris ranch came up from the south to the dam and then disappeared north into the mountains."

"I wonder why they called this spot Condor Castle," Pete said. "I don't see any condors."

"Just as well," said Bob with a chuckle. "A condor is a kind of vulture!"

"Maybe," guessed Diego, "the name comes from the bird's-eye view up here."

"Probably," said Bob. "But let's not worry about the name. We're here to look for the Cortés Sword! Where do you think Don Sebastián hid it?"

"There must be a hiding place up here," answered Pete. "A hollow somewhere, a crack in the rock, maybe even a cave. Let's search, fellows!"

They spread out over the whole top of the rock, but quickly saw there wasn't a hollow or crevice in it. The top was almost as smooth as marble. They stamped on every inch of it, and felt along the sheer sides as far down as they could reach. The rock was completely solid.

"Nobody hid anything in this rock!" said Pete. "Let's try below it, on the sides of the ridge."

Bob nodded. "Okay, Pete, why don't you take the creek side, and Diego and I will go down the arroyo side."

The boys scrambled off the peak and began to search again. Above the now trickling creek, Pete worked his way down the slope, making wider and wider sweeps. He found some loose boulders, but no cracks or hollows, no safe place to hide a sword.

Finally Pete gave up and walked around the north end of the ridge to find the others. Bob and Diego were almost finished searching on their side.

"There just isn't any hole or crack to hide anything in, Second," Bob complained.

Diego added, "Maybe Don Sebastián buried the sword."

"Don't say that!" Pete groaned. "We'd have to dig up the whole ridge. It'd take us forever!"

"I don't think Don Sebastián buried it, Diego," Bob said

slowly. "If Jupiter's theory is right—if Don Sebastián escaped successfully and went to hide the sword—he didn't have a lot of time to work in. Put yourself in his place. He knew he was in danger and might not come back to dig up the sword himself, he knew that José might not return for years, and he knew that Sergeant Brewster and his pals were probably close behind him. If he buried the sword, he'd have to mark the spot clearly for José, or else the sword might never be found. But if he did mark the spot, Sergeant Brewster could see the sign, too, and guess what it meant."

Bob shook his head. "No, I'm sure Don Sebastián wouldn't have buried the sword. He would have hidden it somewhere near Condor Castle—someplace that José would be sure to think of. A place he wouldn't have to take time to get ready, and wouldn't have to mark.

"But," Pete said, looking all around, "where?"

"Well, we're pretty sure the sword isn't on this high ridge by Condor Castle," said Bob. "So think of the rock as only a landmark, a clue to the general area. There must have been someplace nearby that Don Sebastián and José often went to. Diego, is there anywhere—"

"The dam, maybe?" Diego suggested. "It was here then."

"The dam?" Bob said. "Why not?"

Diego led them along the side of the ridge and across the low mound at its end. The mound ran up to the left corner of the dam. Water was spilling over the dam's center gate in a narrow stream, falling thirty feet to the creek bed below. The boys scrambled down the mound and dropped into the creek bed, heedless of wet feet. They examined the whole face of the dam as high as they could reach. It was built of hundreds—maybe thousands—of small boulders, fitted together and caulked with some kind of limestone mortar. There were no loose rocks, holes, or crevices.

"Solid as steel," Pete said.

"My family had it built by local Indians almost two hundred years ago," said Diego.

"Well, they sure didn't leave any cracks to hide a sword in," said Bob, "at least down here at the bottom. If there are cracks farther up, you'd need a ladder to reach them, and Don Sebastián probably didn't have a ladder. But let's try the top."

They scrambled back up the mound, sinking in where the ground was soft from the recent rain, and climbed up to the top of the dam. It was six feet thick at the top, made of the same fitted rocks. But here there were holes and crevices, and the boys split up to search. Half an hour later, they all gave up.

"If the sword is in the dam," Pete said grimly, "we'll have to tear the dam down to find it."

"Don Sebastien didn't have time to make a fancy hiding place," Bob reminded him. "I think we can say the sword isn't in the dam, which means we're at a dead end. We'll have to find a brand-new clue."

"Where, Bob?" asked Pete. "We've been all through those army documents, and Don Sebastián wrote only that one letter around then."

"He was an important man, and he must have had many friends in the area," Bob said. "Perhaps he got help from someone, or perhaps people saw him that day. We need to find something that can tell us more about what he did, maybe even something he said."

"Gee," Diego said doubtfully, "it's been so long, Bob."

"Yes, but back in those days, without the telephone,

people wrote more letters and put more news in them,"
Bob pointed out. "And lots of people kept diaries and
journals. Maybe there was even a newspaper here then.
I bet we can find some good stuff at—"

"I know," Pete moaned. "Back at the Historical Society! Gosh, detective work sure can get boring!"

Bob laughed. "Well, most of the old papers are likely to
be in Spanish, so you'll be spared reading them, Pete!
But we might as well wait till tomorrow, when Jupiter
can help. Besides, I haven't done any homework yet this
weekend."

Pete moaned again. He'd forgotten all about his homework.

The boys started across the top of the dam toward the
road and their bikes. Just as they walked off the dam,
Pete stopped and stood alertly.

"Diego?" the tall boy said, staring off to the right, "does
someone on your ranch own four big, black dogs?"

"Dogs?" Diego said. "No, I—"

"I see them, Second," Bob said, his voice uneasy.

The four big black dogs were some distance away,
above the reservoir and beyond the burned area on the
Alvaro side of the creek. They were pacing wildly in front
of some trees and thick brush, their red tongues lolling
out and their eyes glittering.

"Wow," Bob said nervously, "they sure look mean,
and—"

A shrill whistle seemed to sound from nowhere. Pete
whirled, and pointed back across the dam.

"That's a signal! Run for those trees across the dam!"

In the distance, the four dogs raced toward the dam
with their teeth bared and red tongues dripping! The
boys tumbled back over the dam, and pounded across the

rocky ground toward a line of old oaks some fifty yards away.

"It's . . . too . . . far!" Bob panted.

"We . . . we'll . . . never . . . make it!" Diego gasped.

"Faster, guys!" Pete urged.

"Pete!" Diego cried as he looked back. "They're swimming!"

In their violent pursuit of their quarry, the four dogs had plunged straight into the small reservoir instead of circling it by the faster route across the dam! They were swimming strongly, and were soon out and leaping after the fleeing boys. But the delay had been just enough!

The three boys reached the twisted live oaks, clambered wildly up, and sat on the heavy branches looking down at the four leaping, snarling dogs.

They were trapped!

# 9

# The sheriff makes an arrest

The shrill whistle came again. The dogs stopped snarling and leaping, and lay down under the trees.

"Look!" Bob said. "Skinny and that ranch manager, Cody!"

Their thin enemy and the stocky cowboy were trotting across the dam. Skinny was grinning with delight at the sight of the boys high in the trees. When the two came up, Cody ordered the dogs back sharply. They lay at his heels, alert and quivering, as he looked up at the treed boys. His small eyes sparkled, and he smiled nastily.

"So we've got some trespassers, eh? These trees just happen to be on Norris land!"

"Your dogs chased us here, and you know it!" Diego cried.

"What were you and your dogs doing on Alvaro land!" Pete said hotly.

Cody laughed. "Now how you going to prove that, boy?"

"All I see," Skinny said innocently, "is three trespassers up a tree on my dad's land."

"Like we told the sheriff," Cody said with a smile, "we've been having trouble with trespassers." He nodded toward the dirt road on the Norris side of the creek. A sheriff's car was coming up it. "I guess he'll believe us now."

The sheriff's car parked, and the sheriff himself got out with a deputy. They strode up to Skinny and Cody.

"What's going on here?" the sheriff demanded.

"We've treed some trespassers, Sheriff," Cody said. "The Alvaro kid and two buddies. I told you the Alvaros and their friends act like they think it's still all their land! Running their horses on our land, breaking our fences, making illegal campfires. You know how bad a campfire is out here now."

The sheriff looked up at the boys. "All right, you boys, climb down. Cody, hold those dogs back."

The boys climbed down as Cody controlled the growling dogs. The sheriff looked closely at the two Investigators.

"I know you two, don't I? Pete Crenshaw and Bob Andrews of The Three Investigators! From what Chief Reynolds has told me, you two should know better. Trespassing is a serious matter."

"We weren't trespassing, sir," Bob said quietly. "We were on Alvaro land when those dogs chased us here."

"Oh, sure." Skinny sneered. "They'd have to lie, Sheriff."

"You're the liar, Skinny Norris!" Pete raged.

"Sheriff," Bob went on, "if we were on Mr. Norris's land when those dogs chased us, how come the dogs are soaking wet? It isn't raining just now."

"Wet?" The sheriff looked at the dogs.

"Yes," Bob said firmly, "because they swam the reservoir to chase us, and that pond, and the whole creek above the dam, is on Alvaro land!"

Cody reddened and blustered. "You gonna listen to kids, Sheriff? The dogs got wet earlier, yeah."

"Well," the sheriff said, looking hard at Cody, "those

wet dogs make your story kind of shaky, Cody. I hope the evidence you got me out here to see is better."

"It is," Cody growled. "Come on, I've got it in my wagon down the road."

"What evidence?" Bob asked as Cody and the sheriff walked away down the road.

"Wouldn't you like to know!" Skinny sneered.

The boys and Skinny glared at each other as they waited under the oak trees for the sheriff. When he returned alone some fifteen minutes later, he was carrying a large brown paper bag. He nodded grimly to Diego and the Investigators.

"All right, you boys can go for now. I don't know who's telling the truth, but I've already warned Cody to keep his dogs on his own land, and now I'm warning you not to trespass."

Diego and Pete opened their mouths to protest, but Bob spoke quickly first:

"Yes, sir, we'll remember." Then he added innocently, "Can you tell us what's in that bag, sir?"

"That's none of your business, Bob Andrews," the sheriff snapped. "Now get out of here!"

Reluctantly, the three boys left. They circled the dogs warily, and went back across the dam to the road and their bikes. The rain began to fall heavily again as they rode down the Alvaros' dirt road to the ruins of the hacienda a mile away.

As they passed the ruins, they saw Pico. He was walking slowly around among the burned rooms of the house as if searching for anything that might have been spared by the flames. "Find anything?" called Pete as the boys rode up.

Pico looked up, startled and then embarrassed. "I'm looking for the Cortés Sword," he admitted. "It occurred to me that if Don Sebastián had hidden it, he might have hidden it in the hacienda. And with the house burned out, it might be revealed now. Metal does not burn in a wood fire, so the sword would be easy to find. But," and he looked around at the skeletal walls remaining, "there is no sword here." He kicked angrily at some roof tiles on the floor.

"But Condor Castle is here, Pico!" Diego cried. "We found it!"

The boys quickly reported their discovery of the old map and the location of Condor Castle, and their search of the ridge near the dam. Pico's dark eyes gleamed at first, but slowly faded as the boys had to admit their failure to find any trace of a hiding place near the big rock on the ridge.

"Then what good is your location of Condor Castle? You found nothing! You're no better off than you were."

"No, that's not true," Bob declared. "Next to finding the sword, we've made the most important discovery of all."

"What is that, Bob?" Pico demanded.

"That Don Sebastián did plan to hide the sword for his son José!" Bob said. "Condor Castle was only on the very oldest map. It had nothing to do with where Don Sebastián was or where he lived, so there was no reason to put it on that letter except as a clue. A clue to tell José where to look for something, and the only thing worth all that was the Cortés Sword!"

"Perhaps," Pico acknowledged, "but you still—"

Before Pico could continue, two cars came up the dirt road of the ranch and roared into the hacienda yard. The first was the Norris ranch wagon, and the second was the sheriff's car. Cody and Skinny Norris jumped from the ranch wagon.

"There he is!" Cody cried.

"Don't let him get away!" Skinny called.

The sheriff got out of his car. "I told you two to let me handle this," he said. "He isn't going to run away."

The sheriff still carried the large brown paper bag the boys had seen earlier. He walked slowly up to Pico.

"Pico, I've got to ask where you were on the day of the brush fire."

"Where I was?" Pico frowned. "I was at the fire, as you know. Earlier, I was with Diego at the central school in Rocky Beach."

"Yes, you were seen then. That was around three P.M. Where before that?"

"Before? On the ranch. What is this about, Sheriff?"

"We found how the brush fire started. Someone built a campfire back on the Norris ranch, well before three P.M. That's illegal this time of year, and it wasn't properly put out. The Norris fence was broken—"

Cody burst out, "And we found tracks of your horses!"

"You went after them and started that fire!" Skinny cried.

Pico's voice was cold. "If your fence is broken, and our horses stray onto your land, we go to get them. Good neighbors do that. But I and my friends do not build fires illegally!"

The sheriff opened the paper bag and took out a flat, black sombrero banded with silver *conchos*.

"Do you recognize this hat, Pico?" the sheriff asked.

"Of course," Pico said, "it is mine. I was afraid it had been burned in the fire. I am glad you—"

"You mean you *hoped* it was burned!" Cody snarled.

"I mean, Mr. Cody, what I say. Is that clear?" Pico's eyes blazed as he faced the burly ranch manager.

"Pico?" the sheriff said. "When did you lose the hat?"

"When?" Pico thought a moment. "At the fire, I suppose. I—"

"No," the sheriff said. "You had no hat at the fire. I remember that. So do firemen I've asked."

"Then," Pico said, "I do not know when I lost it."

"Pico, this hat was found at the site of the campfire that started the brush fire."

"Then why isn't it burned?"

"The brush fire moved away from the campfire in just one direction. This hat was on unburned ground nearby."

There was a silence. The sheriff sighed.

"I'm going to have to arrest you, Pico."

Diego cried out, but Pico silenced the boy. He nodded to the sheriff.

"You must do your duty, Sheriff," Pico said quietly, and walked toward the sheriff's car. "Tell Don Emiliano at once!" he called back to Diego.

The sheriff turned to Cody and Skinny. "You two have to come and make your statements."

"You bet we will," Cody said.

"It'll be a pleasure," Skinny added. He laughed at the boys as he followed Cody to their ranch wagon.

Stunned, the Investigators and Diego watched the two cars drive away. There were tears in Diego's eyes as he turned to the boys.

"Pico couldn't have started that fire!" he cried.

"No, of course not," said Bob. "I *know* there's something wrong with the sheriff's story, but I can't think just what. And I *know* I've seen that hat before. But when, and where? Oh, why couldn't Jupiter have been here!"

The slim Investigator sighed with frustration. "Well, now we have two problems to solve, fellows. We must find the Cortés Sword, and we must free Pico!"

# 10

# New ideas

Diego rode off to Emiliano Paz's, and Bob and Pete hurried back to Rocky Beach. The two Investigators tried to call Jupiter for the rest of the day but got no answer at the Jones house. As Jupe had predicted, his great-uncle's birthday party was keeping him away till late. Finally Bob and Pete gave up and went to bed.

As Bob came down the stairs to breakfast the next morning, his father looked up from the morning newspaper.

"I see that your friend Pico Alvaro has been arrested on suspicion of causing a brush fire," Mr. Andrews said. "That's a very serious charge, Bob, and I'm surprised. Alvaro is an experienced rancher. He shouldn't make such a mistake."

"He didn't, Dad! We're sure that the sheriff's made a mistake, or someone is framing Pico, and we're going to prove it!"

"I hope so, son," Mr. Andrews said.

Bob gulped his breakfast and then called Jupiter to report what had happened. Jupiter took the news about Pico poorly.

"Of course Pico didn't set that fire, and you should know why! You could have stopped the sheriff yourself, Bob. Can't you remember anything? We saw Pico's hat ourselves." Jupiter was grumpy because he'd missed all the excitement.

"Well, thanks a lot," replied Bob, stung. "I just don't happen to have a photographic memory like you. So *when* did we see the hat?"

"Oh, I'll tell you at school," said Jupe maddeningly.

"Great," said Bob and slammed down the phone, now in as bad a mood as Jupe.

But the Investigators were too busy at school all day to even talk. Bob and Jupiter both regained their good humor and by the end of school were friends again. Classes ended early, so the boys had most of the afternoon free to pursue their investigation.

"Did anyone see Diego today?" asked Jupiter as the boys biked through more rain to the salvage yard.

"I looked for him, but I didn't see him," said Pete. "I don't think he made it to school."

Diego hadn't. He'd spent the day with Emiliano Paz trying to arrange for a lawyer for Pico. The slim boy was waiting outside Headquarters when the Investigators arrived at the salvage yard. As soon as everyone slipped inside the hidden trailer, Diego filled in the detective team on what was happening.

"We can't afford a private lawyer, so the Public Defender's Office is helping," Diego said. "They say that it doesn't look good for Pico."

"We know he didn't do it, Diego," Bob said angrily.

"But how do we prove it?" Diego said, tears in his eyes. "And how can we save our land now? With Pico in jail he can't do anything. We don't even have enough money for bail!"

"What *is* bail?" asked Pete.

"It's money that you leave with the court as a guarantee

that you'll show up for your trial if you're let out of jail beforehand," said Jupiter. "If you can raise bail, you don't have to wait in jail for hearings to take place or for your trial to start."

"The judge set Pico's bail at five thousand dollars," said Diego.

"Five thousand dollars!" exclaimed Pete. "Hardly anybody has that kind of money!"

"You don't have to put up the whole amount in cash," explained Jupiter. "Only about ten percent. For the rest, you can pledge property—your house, say. Then if you don't show up when you're wanted in court, the court keeps the money and property. If you do show up, you get your bail back. Most people do show up—they don't want to get in even bigger trouble."

Diego nodded. "Pico would show up. His pride would not let him run away. But we haven't got the bail anyway —either the five hundred dollars cash that the judge demanded or the property to pledge for the rest of the bail."

"What about your ranch?" asked Pete.

"That's mortgaged to Don Emiliano, so we can't promise it to the court. We are trying to borrow bail money from friends. But for now, Pico has to stay in jail!"

"I think," Jupiter said grimly, "someone may have counted on that. I don't think that this is an accident. That hat was stolen somehow and put out near the campfire."

"But how do we prove it, Jupiter?" Diego wailed again.

"We don't even know when Pico last had his hat," Bob added.

"But we do know, fellows," announced Jupiter, "that Pico had his hat around three o'clock last Thursday, the day of the brush fire. Don't you remember? He was wearing it when we met him outside school!"

"Of course, of course," cried Bob, striking his forehead.

"And that means that Pico couldn't have left the hat by the campfire! Before three o'clock, he had the hat. After three o'clock, he was with us, and then fighting the fire. If the sheriff is sure Pico didn't have his hat at the fire, then it was lost—or stolen—sometime between our leaving school that day and our arriving at the site of the brush fire!"

"Jupe?" Bob said slowly. "What if Pico lost his hat while we were on the way to the fire? He was riding in the back of the truck. What if the wind blew his hat off and carried it to the campfire?"

"Pico's hat could not blow off," Diego stated. "It has a draw-cord under the chin. Pico always pulls it tight for a ride."

"And there was hardly any wind that day," added Pete. "That's what kept the brush fire from getting out of control."

"Anyway," Jupiter said, "that brush fire was certainly started before we arrived at the ranch. So if the hat blew off in the truck, it wouldn't matter. It would mean that the hat got near the campfire *after* the brush fire started."

"Except," Bob went on in dismay, "we can't really prove it, can we? I mean, *we* know Pico had the hat at three P.M., but it's only our word against that of Cody and Skinny!"

"Well, our word is certainly worth something," said Jupe huffily. "But you're right. We don't have any real proof. So we'll have to find it! We have to discover exactly what did happen to the hat."

"How do we do that, Jupe?" Pete asked.

"The first move, I think, is to talk to Pico and see if he

can remember exactly when he last had his hat," Jupiter decided. "But we must also continue our search for the Cortés Sword. I am convinced that Skinny and Cody know we're looking for the sword, or for something valuable that will help the Alvaros keep their land, and that Pico's arrest is an attempt to stop us!"

"So it's back to the Historical Society to look for any other references to Don Sebastián," Bob said.

Pete groaned. "That could take another hundred years!"

"It won't be fast work, Second," Jupiter conceded, "but not quite that bad. We have just two days to concentrate on—September 15 and 16, 1846. Don Sebastián was a prisoner until he escaped on September 15, and no one ever saw him again. And it was the very next day, September 16, that those three soldiers were found to be missing. No one saw them again, either."

"No one we know about, you mean," Bob said. He leaned forward in his chair. "First, I've been thinking about Condor Castle. We've been assuming that it's a clue to the hiding place of the sword. But maybe it's just what it ought to be up at the top of a letter—Don Sebastián's address!"

Jupiter shook his head. "Don Sebastián's address was the Cabrillo house—or his hacienda."

"Not necessarily," Bob said. "Fellows, I remember reading about a man in the same kind of trouble as Don Sebastián. He was a Scotsman named Cluny MacPherson. When the English invaded the Scottish Highlands in 1745 and beat the Scots at the battle of Culloden, they tried to kill or imprison all the Highland chiefs. Most of the chiefs who escaped fled the country—but not Cluny, the chief of Clan MacPherson. Even though he knew the English were after him, he refused to leave."

"What did he do, Bob?" Diego wondered.

"He lived in a cave right on his own land for almost eleven years!" Bob replied. "His whole clan helped to hide him. They gave him food and water and clothes, and the English never knew where he was until things were safe and he came out on his own!"

"You mean," Pete exclaimed, "you think Condor Castle was a clue to where Don Sebastián himself was going to hide?"

Bob nodded. "You remember how Pico wondered why no one saw Don Sebastián again if he wasn't shot and lost in the ocean? And where he went if he did escape? Well, I think he planned to hide right on his own ranch somewhere near Condor Castle!"

"And his friends would have had to feed him and help him!" Jupiter exclaimed. "You could be right, Records! I overlooked that possibility. If it's true, it gives us something else to look for in old journals and diaries and letters —some mention of hiding food or clothing, of helping someone! But we'll have to extend the period of our search then—say, through the rest of September 1846 for a start."

"Oh, swell," Pete moaned, "more work! Just what we need."

"We need every clue we can find," Jupiter said. "But most of the records will be in Spanish, so Diego and I will have to do the research."

"What will Pete and I do, Jupe?" Bob asked.

"You and Pete will go to the jail and try to make Pico remember what happened to his hat!"

# 11

# A
## visit to jail

The Rocky Beach jail was on the top floor of Police Head-quarters. It was reached by a special corridor and elevator on the first floor. The corridor, which opened to the left of the main entrance to the building, was blocked by a barred gate. A policeman sat at a desk in front of the bars. Bob and Pete stood at the desk nervously, and asked to visit Pico Alvaro.

"Sorry, boys," the policeman at the desk said, "visiting hours are just after lunch—unless you're his lawyers!"

The policeman grinned at them.

"Well," Bob said, trying to look dignified, "he is our client."

"We're sort of something like his lawyers," Pete added.

"All right, boys, I'm too busy to play—"

"We're private detectives, sir," Bob said quickly. "Junior detectives, I mean, but Pico really is our client. We have to talk to him about the case. It's really important. We—"

The policeman scowled. "Okay, that's it! Out, you two!"

Bob and Pete gulped and started to turn away. A voice spoke behind them:

"Show him your cards, boys."

Chief Reynolds of the Rocky Beach Police stood behind Bob and Pete, smiling at them. Bob showed the policeman at the desk their two cards. The man read them slowly.

"What do you want here, boys?" Chief Reynolds asked. They told him, and he nodded seriously.

"Well," the chief said, "I think we might stretch a point in this case. Pico Alvaro isn't exactly a dangerous criminal, Sergeant, and investigators do have a right to see their client."

"Yes, sir," the police sergeant at the desk said. "I didn't know they were friends of yours."

"Not friends, Sergeant, civilian helpers. You'd be surprised how many times the boys have really helped us."

The chief smiled at Bob and Pete again, and walked away. The policeman at the desk pressed a buzzer. Behind the barred gate, another policeman came out of an office into the corridor and unlocked the gate from inside. The boys hurried through, jumping nervously as the gate clanged shut behind them.

"Wow," Pete said, "I'm sure glad we're just visitors!"

The boys went down the corridor to an elevator, rode up, and got out on the top floor. They emerged into a long, brightly lighted corridor lined with desks and open counters. The first counter to the left was where prisoners emptied their pockets and left all their personal possessions. The next counter was where they were fingerprinted, and at the third counter they were given jail clothes, which they changed into in a locker room at the far end of the corridor on the left. Across from the locker room was a barred door marked Visiting Room. Then, along the rest of the right-hand side of the corridor, were desks. Policemen sat at some of them interrogating prisoners about to be jailed.

"Over here, boys," a policeman called from the first

desk. "You're Andrews and Crenshaw? Private detectives?"

They nodded, swallowing. The officer typed their names and addresses on printed forms, then entered the name of the prisoner they were visiting and the nature of their business.

"Okay, stand over against that wall."

Bob and Pete stood against the wall, and another officer searched them quickly and expertly for concealed weapons or anything else that might help a prisoner escape. Pete was glad that he wasn't carrying his Swiss Army knife that day. Then the first policeman took the boys down to the barred visitors door, unlocked it, and sent them inside.

They saw a long, narrow room with a low, solid counter dividing the room lengthwise. On the counter was a double row of three-sided, desklike cubicles. One set of cubicles opened toward the visitors' door, and the second set opened toward the far wall, which contained a barred door that led into the jail itself. When seated at a cubicle, you looked over a chin-high barrier at the cubicle on the other side. A visitor and a prisoner could thus see and talk to each other in facing cubicles, but could not pass anything over the barrier between them without being spotted by the policeman who sat in the room.

Bob and Pete sat down in one of the cubicles. Soon the door on the prisoner's side opened and a guard brought Pico in. Pico sat facing the boys across the chin-high barrier.

"It is good of you to visit," he said quietly, "but there is nothing I need."

"We know you didn't make that campfire!" Pete exclaimed.

Pico smiled. "I, too, know that. Unfortunately, the sheriff does not."

"But we think we can prove it," Bob said.

"Prove it? How, boys?"

They told Pico all they had realized about the hat.

"So," Bob explained, "at three P.M. you were still wearing the hat at the school in Rocky Beach. You couldn't have left the hat near that campfire on the Norris ranch until after we all got to the hacienda. And by that time, the fire had already started—set by someone else!"

"Then," Pico said, his eyes gleaming, "my hat must have gotten on the Norris land *after* the fire started! Excellent, boys! You are very good detectives indeed. Yes, my hat must have gotten out there accidentally, or—"

"Or," Bob finished, "someone put it out there on purpose!"

"So that I would be falsely accused." Pico nodded. "But you cannot prove that I was wearing my hat at the school. It is only your word."

"Yes," Bob agreed, "but we know the truth, and now we have to find out how the hat got out there near that campfire."

"So we have to know where you left it," Pete said. "You were wearing it at the school, and I think I remember it at the salvage yard. Were you wearing it in the truck?"

"The truck?" Pico frowned. "We were all in the back, yes. I talked about our family. Perhaps . . . No, I can't be sure. I don't remember taking the hat off, or even wearing it!"

"You have to remember!" Pete said fiercely.

"*Think!*" Bob urged.

But Pico only looked at them helplessly.

Diego sighed wearily as he turned the microfilm reader to another page of the old newspaper he was skimming. He was in the Rocky Beach Public Library, where Jupe had sent him when they discovered that the Historical Society didn't have a full collection of old newspapers. Diego had gone through two months' worth of issues of the weekly newspaper published in Rocky Beach in 1846. He was now up to the fourth week in October. So far he had found very little. There was nothing about Don Sebastián at all except for a brief mention of his death. The account was clearly based on Sergeant Brewster's report and said nothing new.

Diego sighed again, and stretched. The reading room was silent except for the steady sound of the falling rain outside. He turned to the small stack of books on the table beside him. They were all printed memoirs and diaries of local residents in the nineteenth century.

Diego opened the first memoir and began to look for entries from mid-September 1846.

Jupiter closed the fifth journal he had read and listened to the rain outside the Historical Society. The old handwritten journals of the Spanish settlers were fascinating, and he had to keep reminding himself to read only entries for the dates near the escape of Don Sebastián. But so far even the entries for those violent days of September 1846 had given him no clues.

Dispirited, he opened the sixth journal without much hope. At least he wouldn't have to work so hard to read this one. The sixth journal was in English, one kept by a second lieutenant of cavalry in Frémont's small force of American invaders.

Jupiter located the pages for mid-September and began to read fast.

Some ten minutes later he suddenly leaned forward, his eyes bright and excited, and carefully reread a page in the journal of the long-forgotten second lieutenant.

Then he jumped up, made a copy of the page, returned the old journals to the historian, and hurried out into the rain.

Pico shook his head again in the visitor's room of the Rocky Beach jail.

"I cannot remember, boys. I'm sorry."

"All right," Bob said calmly. "Let's go over it step by step. Now, you were wearing the hat at the school. Jupiter remembers that clearly, and I think I do. Now—"

"I'll bet Skinny and even that Cody remember Pico wearing the hat at the school, if they'd admit it," Pete said bitterly.

"But they won't," Bob said. "Pete's pretty sure you were still wearing the hat at the salvage yard. In the truck you told us about the Alvaro land grant. I remember you pointed to things, so you weren't holding the hat in your hand. It was windy and chilly in the truck, so you were probably wearing the hat to keep your head warm."

"Then we got to the hacienda," Pete went on. "We all got out of the truck, and you talked to Uncle Titus about the statue of Cortés. Then what, Pico? Did you go into the hacienda and maybe take off your hat?"

"Well, I . . ." Pico thought hard. "No, I did not go into the house. I . . . we all . . . Wait! Yes, I think I remember!"

"What?" Pete cried.

"Go on," Bob urged.

Pico's eyes gleamed. "We all went straight into the barn to look at the things I was to sell to Mr. Jones. It was dim in the barn and my hat brim shaded my eyes. So I took off the hat to see better, and ..." The tall Alvaro brother looked at the boys. "And I hung it on a peg just inside the barn door! Yes, I am sure. I hung it in the barn, and then when Huerta and Guerra called 'Fire!' I ran out with all of you and left the hat in the barn!"

"Then that's where it should have been, not at the campfire on the Norris ranch," Bob said.

"So someone swiped it from the barn before the barn caught on fire," Pete said, "and put it out at the campfire to frame Pico!"

"But," Pico said slowly, "we still do not have proof."

"Maybe we can find some evidence at the barn, if everything wasn't all burned!" Bob said. "Let's go and tell Jupe, Pete."

The boys said good-bye to Pico, and hurried out as the guard took Pico back to his cell in the jail.

Out in the rain, they rode straight to the Historical Society and ran inside. Jupiter wasn't there!

"Where'd he go, Records?" Pete wondered.

"I don't know," Bob said, biting his lip. "But we've got a couple of hours before dark, Second. There's time to go look for some evidence in the Alvaro barn that someone stole Pico's hat."

"Let's go then," Pete decided. "Maybe Jupe went out there with Diego anyway."

They ran back to their bikes, and peddled swiftly through the steady rain out toward the burned Alvaro hacienda.

# 12

# A discovery in the ruins

The rain stopped as Bob and Pete rode into the hacienda yard. The blackened ruins were silent and deserted, looking like the jagged skeletons of buildings on some battlefield. On the ridge behind the hacienda, the statue of the headless horse loomed eerie and menacing against the low, scudding clouds. Jupiter and Diego weren't anywhere around.

"Maybe we should wait, Records," Pete suggested.

"Well," Bob said, "we're here now. I guess we could look around and see if we can find any clues."

Pete stared at the broken walls and fallen beams of the old barn. "Gosh, it's some mess. Where do we start?"

"I think," Bob replied slowly, "Jupe would say first things first. We should look outside the barn for anything that might have been dropped, or maybe for some footprints."

Pete nodded, and they spread out on either side of the corral in front of the barn. Bent low, and peering at every inch of the soggy ground, they worked their way slowly across the corral toward the entrance to the barn. The days of rain had turned the whole yard into a slick and sticky clay mud. It covered their shoes and made uneasy sucking sounds as they moved.

They met in front of what had once been the barn door.

All that remained of it was a charred door frame, twisted and leaning crazily.

"Not even a twig on the ground," Pete groaned. "The mud's so deep it'd probably cover anything smaller than a boulder anyway."

"And I don't think there would have been any footprints even before the rain. Adobe soil is hard as a rock when it's dry," Bob said. "Let's try inside."

Inside, the burned barn was a terrible mess of fallen roof timbers, collapsed walls, the remnants of rooms and stalls, and the blackened jumble of the hundreds of valuable items the Alvaros had been going to sell to Uncle Titus. Two of the outer walls had fallen in completely, and the other two were only skeletons. The windows in the standing walls looked like gaping wounds. After days of rain, the stench of the burned debris was terrible. Almost nothing in the barn was recognizable. The boys stood and looked at the confusion.

"How do we find anything in here?" Pete moaned. "I mean, we don't even know what we're looking for."

"We're looking for anything that could give us a clue to who was here and took Pico's hat," Bob said, refusing to be so easily daunted. "And you know what Jupe would say—we'll know it when we see it!"

"Swell," Pete said, "but just how do we find anything in this wreck, and where do we start to look?"

"We start where the hat was last known to be," Bob declared, and pointed to the side of the doorframe. The front wall was one of the two walls still standing. "Look, the peg Pico hung his hat on is still there on what's left of that wall."

"What's left of the peg," Pete muttered, but followed Bob to the wall.

A row of three pegs just inside the door had been burned to stubs, but they were still visible on a blackened wall stud. Bob and Pete began to search the ground beneath the pegs.

The floor was a jumbled litter of wood ashes and burned debris. Aside from roof tiles, it was hard to be sure of what anything was. The boys found hundreds of small, broken, and blackened pieces as they moved away from the wall in a widening circle, but nothing that seemed to mean anything, or belong to anyone except the Alvaros.

Pete finally sat down on a fallen roof beam. "If there's a clue, it needs a sign on it," he said.

"I guess you're right, Second," Bob admitted reluctantly. "There are so many pieces of broken—"

"Hey, someone's coming," Pete said. He got up and hurried toward the door. "It must be Jupe and Diego. Ju—" He jumped back out of sight against the burned wall, his voice a sharp whisper. "Bob! It's three guys! Strangers!"

Bob crouched behind a mound of debris and peered out the door.

"They're coming toward the barn! I don't like the look of them, Second. Quick, over there under those beams! Hurry."

They scurried quickly but silently to one side of the barn. Here, the side wall had fallen in over some roof beams that leaned up against the front wall. Underneath the beams was a small, dark, triangular space. The boys crawled into it, then lay on the ground and looked outward. Careful to make no sound, they barely breathed.

Moments later the three men came into the barn.

"Wow," Pete whispered uneasily, "they look mean."

The three men stood just inside the door, looking around at the ruins. One was a big, black-haired man with a thick mustache and three days' growth of black stubble on his heavy face. The second was small and skinny, with a narrow, ratlike face and mean little eyes. The third was fat and bald with a big red nose and broken front teeth. They were all dirty and rough looking, and dressed like saddle-tramp cowboys in worn jeans, muddy cowboy boots, work shirts, and greasy, battered Stetson hats. Their rough hands and faces looked as if they hadn't been washed for a month.

None of the men looked happy as they stared at the ruins.

"We ain't gonna find nothin' in here," the small, skinny man said. "How we find anythin' here, Cap?"

"We gotta find 'em," said the big, black-haired man with the mustache.

"No way, Cap," the fat one said in a high, squeaky voice. He shook his big head back and forth. "No way, no sir."

"Just you all look, you hear?" Cap said. "They gotta be right aroun' here."

"Sure, Cap," the fat one squeaked. He began to kick at the debris, peering expectantly at the floor as if whatever they were looking for would appear any second.

The small, ratlike man began to walk around looking here and there, but not too hard. The big one, Cap, swore at him.

"Get down and look, Pike, you ain't pickin' daisies!"

The skinny Pike glared at Cap for a moment, then bent lower and began to search harder. Cap turned toward the fat one.

"You, too, Tulsa. We'll each take a section, you got that?"

Tulsa immediately dropped to his hands and knees in the ashes and began to crawl around with his fat face almost touching the floor. Cap and Pike stared at him in disgust for a moment, and then fanned out to search on either side of the leaning door frame.

"You sure they was lost in here, Cap?" Pike asked.

"Sure, I'm sure. We had to jump the ignition to get out of here that day, didn't we? Had to go get another set later."

Twice as the three men searched the ruins, one of them passed close to where Bob and Pete lay hidden and holding their breath. The big, black-haired Cap was so close the boys could have touched his boots. Pete gulped, and silently pointed to a thin-bladed, heavy-hilted knife sheathed in Cap's boot!

"I don' know," the skinny Pike said after a time. "Who says they wasn't lost somewhere's else before?"

"We had 'em to drive here, didn't we, stupid?" Cap said in disgust.

"Okay, so maybe they got dropped outside!" Pike shot back.

The skinny little man sat down on a beam right over Bob and Pete! With another ugly-looking sheath knife he began to whittle at a burned splinter of wood.

"Okay," Cap finally conceded, "maybe you're right. I guess we ain't gonna find 'em in here without a light anyhow. Let's go look where we was parked that day, and if we don't find 'em, we'll go get some lights."

As the boys tried to not even breathe, Pike jumped up and hurried out of the ruined barn with the other two. Bob and Pete listened for a time without moving. They could hear the three men talking and arguing out in the muddy yard. Bob and Pete waited. Then there was silence outside. Cautiously, they crept out from under the collapsed wall and slipped to the door. The yard was empty. Bob turned to Pete with his eyes gleaming.

"I don't know who they are, Second," he said, "but I've got a hunch they were here the day of the fire and probably had something to do with Pico's hat! I think they lost some car keys!"

"That's what it sounded like," Pete agreed. "They look like cowboys. Maybe they work for Mr. Norris!"

Bob added, "They sure want to find those keys, and that means the keys are dangerous to them—or to someone! Let's look hard!"

"We already did, Records," Pete pointed out. "Those guys couldn't find them, either."

"They didn't look very hard, and now we know what we're looking for," Bob said. "I saw a burned rake over there—go get it! We'll rake up the debris around the peg!"

Pete found the rake in a corner. Its handle had been burned half away, but the metal part was still usable. He began to rake through the ashes and debris. Every time the rake struck something metallic, he and Bob bent over excitedly to examine the object. Their search was a little easier than before because the day had brightened, letting more light into the roofless barn. The clouds were breaking up and patches of blue showed overhead.

Finally Bob cried, "Pete!" and pointed down. Something glinted in the light.

Pete raked it up. The two boys almost bumped heads as they both bent over to pick it up.

"Two keys on a chain with a silver dollar!" Bob cried.

"Any marks on them? Identification?" Pete asked quickly.

Bob looked. "No, nothing. But they're car keys, all right, and they've got to be what those men were looking for."

"Unless they're Pico's," Pete said. "Or maybe they belong to one of those friends of his."

*"Hey! You two kids!"*

Bob and Pete whirled. The fat man named Tulsa stared at them from the burned doorway. For a moment he didn't seem to know what to do.

"Out the back!" Pete whispered to Bob.

They ran out the rear of the ruined building, and got behind some live oaks that grew in back of the barn. Then darting from tree to tree, they moved to a position from which they could look back into the hacienda yard.

"You, there!"

The big, black-haired man named Cap stood near the ruined hacienda, gesturing at the boys. Suddenly, the rat-like little man came out of the corral and called to him.

"Cap! Tulsa says those kids found somethin' in the barn!"

The two boys looked wildly around. They were blocked from their bikes back in the hacienda yard, and there was no place nearby to hide!

"The ridge!" Pete hissed.

They fled toward the high ridge where the headless horse statue loomed against the sky!

# 13

# Danger on the ranch

When Jupiter left the Historical Society, he rode to the library and found Diego. The slender young Alvaro boy was looking gloomy.

"There's a lot in the old newspapers about shoot-outs in the canyons around that time," he reported, "but nothing that helps us figure out what happened to Don Sebastián."

"Never mind now," Jupiter said eagerly. "I think I've found something! Bob and Pete should be finished at the jail by now—they'll probably be at Headquarters. Come on!"

The boys rode quickly through the rain to the salvage yard. To avoid being seen by Aunt Mathilda or Uncle Titus and perhaps grabbed for some chore, Jupiter led Diego in the back way. He stopped his bike along the rear fence about fifty feet from the corner. The entire fence around the salvage yard had been decorated by Rocky Beach artists, and Jupe had halted in front of a dramatic scene of the San Francisco fire of 1906. A little dog sat in the painting near a red spout of flame.

"We named the dog Rover," Jupiter informed Diego, "so this secret entrance is called Red Gate Rover!"

One of the little dog's eyes was a knot in a board. Jupiter carefully pulled out the knot and reached in to release a hidden catch. Three boards in the fence swung up, and

Diego and Jupiter slipped into the salvage yard.

Once inside, they parked their bikes and crawled through hidden passages in the junk piles until they reached a panel that opened directly into Headquarters. Bob and Pete weren't there.

"They're probably still talking to Pico," Jupiter said. "We'll wait."

"All right," Diego said, "but what did you discover?"

Jupiter took out a piece of paper. His eyes gleamed.

"A second lieutenant who came here—one of Frémont's men—kept a journal. I found this entry for September 15, 1846," Jupiter explained, and began to read. " 'My senses are in a whirl! I fear the strain of our invasion has affected my mind. Tonight I was ordered out to the hacienda of Don Sebastián Alvaro to search for hidden contraband. Just at dusk, I saw what can only have been the figment of a deluded mind. On a ridge across what the local people call Santa Inez Creek I clearly observed Don Sebastián Alvaro himself leading his horse and flourishing his great sword! Before I could attempt to cross the creek total darkness engulfed me, and not wanting to risk an encounter alone at night, I returned to our camp. There I was informed that Don Sebastián Alvaro had been shot and killed trying to escape from us that very morning! What, then, did I see across the creek as I left the Alvaro hacienda? A specter? An illusion? Had I heard some casual reference to Don Sebastián's death and not remembered until the Alvaro hacienda dredged it from the depths of my tired mind? I cannot say.' "

"But Don Sebastián wasn't shot!" Diego cried eagerly. "So that lieutenant really did see him! And, Jupiter, he had the sword!"

"Yes," Jupiter agreed triumphantly, "I believe we have

now proved conclusively that Don Sebastián was alive on the night of September 15, and that he did have the Cortés Sword with him after he escaped. There was nothing wrong with that lieutenant's mind or eyes. The moment Bob and Pete arrive, we'll go out and investigate the spot the lieutenant described!"

But after half an hour Bob and Pete still had not appeared at Headquarters. Diego became alarmed.

"Could something have happened to them, or to Pico?" the slim boy asked uneasily.

"That is always possible," Jupiter acknowledged grimly, "but I think it is more probable that they learned something from Pico and went to investigate on their own."

"But where would they go?"

"Considering that their task was to question Pico about where he had last seen his hat, I suspect that they have gone to your hacienda. Let's go find them."

Jupiter and Diego slipped back out through Red Gate Rover and rode their bicycles as fast as they could out to the burned hacienda. The rain had stopped and the sky slowly brightened. Santa Inez Creek was running full and high when the boys crossed it on the stone bridge of the county road. Passing the rank of ridges between the creek and the arroyo, they glanced up at the headless Cortés statue high on the last ridge.

"Jupiter! The statue! It's . . . it's moving!" Diego cried.

They slammed on the brakes of their bikes and stared up at the statue.

"No, it's not moving!" Jupiter said. "There's someone up there near it!"

"Someone hiding behind the statue!" Diego cried.

"There's two of them. "They're running now!"

"Coming this way down the ridge!"

"It's Bob and Pete!"

"Come on!"

They shoved their bikes into the brush beside the road and ran forward. Bob and Pete were slipping and sliding down the end of the ridge toward the road. Out of breath and panting, the four boys met where the ridge ended in a deep ditch beside the pavement.

"We found some evidence, First!" Pete panted.

"And three guys found us!" Bob gasped.

"What three guys, fellows?" Diego asked breathlessly.

"We don't know, but they're after us right now!"

"Back to the bridge," Jupiter puffed. "We'll hide under it!"

"They're sure to look there, Jupe!" Bob objected.

"There's a big drain pipe back down the road!" Diego cried. "It runs into this ditch, and it's all overgrown! Come on!"

They raced back along the muddy brush-filled ditch. Diego scrambled amidst thick and thorny chaparral to uncover the mouth of a giant drainage pipe that came out of a hillside. The boys tumbled inside the pipe despite a thin stream of draining rain water, and pulled the brush back across the mouth. Huddled together, they waited anxiously.

"What evidence was it you found?" Jupiter whispered.

Bob and Pete told him about the set of keys and their adventures in the burned barn. Diego looked at the keys in the dim light of the pipe.

"I am sure they aren't ours," he said.

"Those men said they lost them and had to jump the ignition of some car?" Jupiter pondered. "From the way you tell it, fellows, it sounds as if they were at the barn *before* it burned. And they obviously don't want anyone to find the keys and know they were there! Perhaps *they* stole the hat and planted it out at that campfire!"

"But who are they, First?" Pete wondered hoarsely.

"I don't know, Second, but somehow they must be in-volved with the fire and Pico's arrest. I . . . Shhhhh!"

In the pipe they all fell silent. Running feet were com-ing along the road! The boys peered through the thick bushes and saw the three saddle-tramp cowboys! Grim and silent, the three menacing men trotted past.

Diego whispered, "I never saw them before! If they work for Mr. Norris, they're new."

"Then what are they doing here?" Pete asked.

"That is something we must learn, Second," Jupiter said.

"All I know," Bob said, "is I hope they don't come back!"

The four boys waited, listening hard. Down the road there was only silence. After another fifteen minutes, Jupi-ter sighed nervously.

"I guess one of us had better look," he said.

"I'll go," Diego said. "They're after Bob and Pete, not me. And I live out here, so they might not be suspicious."

The slim boy slipped out quickly so that there would be little chance of anyone seeing where he came from. He climbed up to the road, turned left, and disappeared to-ward the bridge. In the pipe The Three Investigators waited again. Bob was the first to hear someone coming back. He started to go out.

"Wait!" Pete whispered. "Maybe it's not Diego!"

They waited. Someone stopped in front of the pipe.

"Okay, fellows, it's all clear."

It was Diego! The Investigators piled out, and Diego led them back to the bridge over Santa Inez Creek. He pointed toward the mountains. Far ahead, the three cow-boys were disappearing north along the dirt road of the Norris ranch.

"They gave up," Diego said with a grin. "And this is just about where we want to investigate, isn't it, Jupiter?"

"Investigate what?" Bob and Pete asked together.

Jupiter told them about the lieutenant's journal, and showed them the page he had duplicated from it.

"Wow!" Pete exclaimed. "Don Sebastián really did escape! And he must have had the Cortés Sword with him!"

"I'm sure he did," Jupiter said, and he sighed. "But what that lieutenant wrote isn't going to help us find it!"

"But, Jupiter, he wrote—" Diego began in protest.

"He couldn't have seen what he said he did," Jupiter interrupted, "or, at least, where he saw it. Look, he wrote that he was *leaving* the hacienda, so that means he was on our side of the creek, the west side. He looked east, across the creek, from right about here. He says he saw a ridge—but from here there aren't any ridges at all on the other side of the creek!"

On the far side of the swollen creek, as far as the boys could see, the land was flat all the way past the Norris ranch buildings!

"Somehow," Jupiter said gloomily, "he must have made a mistake—about where he was, or in what he remembered when he wrote in his journal."

The boys looked at each other unhappily.

"I guess it's a dead end, fellows," Jupiter said.

Dejected, they walked toward their bikes to ride home.

# 14

# Time runs out for the Alvaros

It started to rain hard again that night, and poured down all the next day. The Investigators had no time to talk about the Cortés Sword or to try to identify the car keys from the burned barn. After classes, they were busy with school activities all afternoon.

"We don't have any new leads anyway," Pete said sadly.

Diego visited Pico in the afternoon and showed his brother the keys. He described the three mysterious cowboys to Pico. But Pico didn't recognize the keys, and he had no idea who the three strangers were or why they were interested in the ruined barn.

"Unless," the older Alvaro said bitterly, "Mr. Norris has hired toughs to force us off our ranch!"

After their dinners that night, The Three Investigators returned to the library and the Historical Society. They searched through the old newspapers, journals, diaries, memoirs, and U.S. Army reports again. They reread the false report of Don Sebastián's death, the statement declaring Sergeant Brewster and his two confederates to be deserters, Don Sebastián's baffling letter with its heading of "Condor Castle," and the American lieutenant's apparently erroneous journal entry. The boys could find nothing new that seemed important.

Rain continued to come down all that night, and all day on Wednesday. Flood warnings went up in the county. After school, Bob and Pete both had chores to do at home. Diego went to visit Pico again, and Jupiter wearily returned to the Historical Society to continue the plodding detective work.

Their chores completed, Bob and Pete met at Headquarters. They took off their wet rain gear and huddled around the small electric heater in the hidden house trailer to wait for Diego and Jupiter.

"You think we're ever going to find that sword, Bob?" Pete asked.

"I don't know, Second," Bob admitted. "If only it all hadn't happened so long ago. There are all kinds of reports of shooting and running around back in the hills, by the Mexican locals and the U.S. Army, but we can't tell if any of them involved Don Sebastián or those three deserters."

Diego came climbing up out of the trap door from Tunnel Two. The slender boy looked even more miserable than he had the last two days. Pete and Bob stared at him in alarm.

"Has something happened to Pico?" Bob cried.

"Is he in more trouble?" Pete echoed.

"Nothing has happened to Pico, but he is in more trouble. We all are."

The unhappy boy took off his wet jacket and sat beside the two Investigators close to the glowing heater. He shook his head hopelessly.

"Señor Paz has sold our mortgage to Mr. Norris," he said.

"Oh, no!" Pete groaned.

"But," Bob said, "he promised to delay as long as—"

"It is not Don Emiliano's fault," Diego said. "He must have his money, and with Pico in jail there is no way we could hope to pay him for a long time. And, Pico needs money for bail and for his defense. Pico told Don Emiliano he must sell now."

"We're sorry, Diego," Bob said quietly.

"Gosh," Pete said, "it sure looks hopeless. I mean, we'll never find that sword without more clues, and now there isn't much time to hunt for them. How long do you think we—"

There was a sudden banging and scrambling outside the panel that led to Red Gate Rover. Jupiter came tumbling in through the panel, wet and puffing.

"Skinny was tailing me!" the stout leader announced, out of breath, "but I eluded him and sneaked through Red Gate Rover without being seen!"

"Why was he chasing you?" Diego wondered.

"I didn't stop to ask him," Jupiter said bluntly. "He may have just wanted to talk, but I wanted to get here, and didn't need to waste time talking with Skinny! Fellows, I've found—"

There was a loud crash as something heavy fell into the mounds of junk around the hidden trailer. Then another crash sounded nearby, somewhere else in the salvage yard. Skinny's voice came to them from out in the rain:

"I know you're around here somewhere, Fatso Jones! You're all around here somewhere, I bet! Think you're so smart!"

Another crash! Skinny was standing out in the rain-soaked salvage yard hurdling heavy objects against all the mounds of junk, knowing the Investigators were hidden somewhere but not sure where.

"Well, you're not so smart, you hear?" Skinny yelled in the rain. "We've got your Mexican pals now, smart guys! Saturday we take over their ranch! You hear that?"

The four boys in the trailer looked at each other. Only

Jupiter seemed puzzled. The others hadn't told him yet about Emiliano Paz selling the mortgage.

"Saturday, that's all!" Skinny shouted. "No way you're gonna help those wetbacks now! It doesn't matter anymore what you think you're up to! This time you're beaten, big shots!" Skinny laughed nastily. "So pleasant dreams, punks! Pleasant dreams!"

For a time they could hear Skinny's laugh as it slowly faded away in the salvage yard. Then there was only the drumming of rain on the trailer's roof.

Jupiter fumed. "Skinny and his dumb bravado! He just wants to make us think—"

"No," Diego said. "This time he's right, Jupiter."

He told the stout First Investigator about Emiliano Paz selling the mortgage to Mr. Norris.

"Our payment is due on Saturday," Diego said glumly. "Don Emiliano would have let us pay part of it, but if we don't pay Mr. Norris in full he can foreclose the mortgage and take the ranch."

"So," Jupiter said, "Mr. Norris appears to have won."

"Jupe!" Bob cried.

"You're not going to just quit!" Pete exclaimed.

"I—I would not blame you," Diego stammered.

Jupiter's eyes flashed. "I said that Mr. Norris *appeared* to have won! That could mean that no one will try to stop us anymore. We must make the most of all the time we have left—and we don't have much!"

"No time," Pete moaned, "and no clues!"

"On the contrary," Jupiter declared. "We have many clues. We simply haven't yet interpreted them correctly. And I have just found still another proof that our speculations *are* correct."

The stout leader of the team took a paper from his

pocket. "Bob was right when he suggested that Don Sebastián might have planned to hide *himself* out in the hills as well as the Cortés Sword. He planned to do it, and he did do it."

He handed the paper to Diego. "It's in Spanish, Diego, and I'm not sure I've got it exactly right. Read it out for us in English."

Diego nodded. "It's from a diary, I guess. The date's September 15, 1846. 'This night word came to our small group of patriots that the eagle has found a nest. We must plan for the care of our most noble bird. Predators are everywhere, it will not be simple, but perhaps now there is something to be done!' " Diego looked up. "You think that the eagle was Don Sebastián, Jupiter? That this entry means that local patriots escaped, and planned to help him to stay hidden?"

"I'm sure of it," Jupiter said. "That diary belonged to the local Spanish mayor then, a personal friend of the Alvaros, and in my reading I learned that Don Sebastián was nicknamed 'The Eagle' in his young days!"

"But," Bob said, looking at the paper with the Spanish writing on it, "how does this help us, First? I mean, maybe I was right and Don Sebastián did hide out like Cluny MacPherson, but this entry doesn't say where. What about later entries in the mayor's diary, Jupe? Do they help?"

"This entry was on the last page of the diary, Bob, and there wasn't a second diary of the mayor's. He was killed a few weeks later fighting the invaders. I guess he got too busy to write."

"Well, if Don Sebastián did hide out in the hills," Pete said, "what happened to him? Maybe his friends helped him to escape out of the area, and he took the sword with him and never came back!"

"That is possible, Second," Jupiter admitted. "It has been all along—but I don't think that happened. If it had, I'm sure there would have been some reference to it in all the diaries and memoirs we've read. No, fellows, I don't think Don Sebastián escaped for good. I think something happened to him out in the mountains, but I don't know what, and I don't think anyone else knew back then either! I think that is the key to the whole mystery—what did happen to Don Sebastián!"

"If they didn't know back then," Pete said, "how do we find out?"

"We find out, Second, because we *do* know where he planned to hide!" Jupiter declared. "He told us when he headed his letter 'Condor Castle'! I'm convinced that the answer is out there near that great rock. There is something out there that we've missed, and right after school tomorrow we're going to go out and find it!"

# 15

# The hiding place

When school let out that Thursday the rain had slackened a little, and the four boys made good time out to the ruins of the hacienda. Alert, they watched carefully for any sign of the three tramplike cowboys.

The dirt road into the mountains was a quagmire after the whole week of rain, so they left their bikes under a makeshift shelter of burned boards. Bob had brought a saddlebag with tools and a flashlight, which he took off his bike and hitched to his belt. The boys started to walk up toward the dam and the great rock of Condor Castle.

"If it gets any wetter, we can swim back," Pete moaned.

They walked off the road through the chaparral and over the rocky ground as much as they could, so their shoes didn't get too muddy. When they got close to the high rocky ridge of Condor Castle, they found the arroyo was too full of water to cross. They had to go around the end of it to get on the ridge, climbing over the mound that separated the arroyo from Santa Inez Creek.

A lot of brush had washed loose from the soft dirt of the mound. Slogging through the mud, the boys reached the ridge, only to have their feet sink into its lower slope as they climbed.

From the top of the giant rock of Condor Castle, the four boys had an awesome view. Above the dam Santa Inez Creek was far over its banks, spreading out across the burned land. At the dam itself, water poured not only through the center gate but also over the whole top, forming a great waterfall. Below the dam the creek boiled and surged high against the mound at the base of the ridge, then flowed in a torrent down toward the county road and the distant ocean.

But the awesome view wasn't what Jupiter had on his mind.

"Where," he said, looking all around, "could a man hide to be sheltered, relatively safe, and more-or-less comfortable for a long time—if he had friends to help him?"

"Not on this ridge, that's for sure," said Pete. "We were all over it the other day and couldn't even find a crack."

"Are there any caves around here, Diego?" Bob asked.

"None that I know of," Diego said. "Maybe far back in the mountains."

"No," Jupiter shook his head. "I'm sure the place must be close."

"Maybe the dam's hollow," Pete suggested.

"Very funny, Second," Bob said.

"Perhaps," Jupiter said, "there's a secret, hidden canyon were a tent or lean-to could have been erected?"

"There's nowhere like that, Jupiter," Diego said. "I've been all over these hills."

"What about tenant houses? For the workers back then!" Bob speculated. "Don Sebastián must have had workers."

"Yes," Diego agreed, "but all the houses were down near where the county road is, on good land. Anyway, they're gone."

"Diego?" Pete said. "Where does the other fork in your dirt road go? The fork that doesn't come here to the dam?"

"Just back deeper into the mountains, then curves back out to the county road on Señor Paz's land."

Pete pointed away from the dam and creek to the far side of the arroyo. "Does that path over there join the other fork?"

"Path?" Jupiter squinted, trying to see where Pete pointed.

"Yeah, over there. It goes away from the dirt road and off around that hill."

They all saw the narrow trail that cut through the chaparral and disappeared among low oak trees around the slope of a hill.

"The shack!" Diego cried. "I forgot about it! There's an old line shack back in there, for the vaqueros on roundup in the old days. It's just boards and tin. I haven't been near it for a long time."

"Was it there in Don Sebastián's time?" Jupiter asked.

"Oh, yes. At least, Pico told me there's always been some sort of shack there. In the old days, it was an adobe room."

"Almost hidden, not used much, and the path to it can be seen from Condor Castle!" Jupiter exclaimed, staring across the arroyo. "That could be the place!"

They climbed down from the giant rock, sinking into the soft earth as they slid down the lower slope and crossed the mound above the arroyo.

Jupiter looked nervously back at the overflowing dam.

"I assume the dam will hold," he said. The unathletic leader wasn't the world's greatest swimmer.

"It always has," Diego said. "Of course, it's pretty old."

"That's real encouraging," Pete muttered.

On the other side of the muddy road, the boys followed the narrow trail through low oaks and thick chaparral. It was heavily overgrown from lack of use. Crossing the rocky shoulder of a hill, the path led into a small canyon nestled between two bigger hills. The canyon was dark and shadowy on the gray day.

"There, fellows!" Diego pointed.

A tiny, ramshackle hut was tucked in under a massive rock overhang, almost invisible behind trees and high brush. The flat roof was made of thin, rusted sheet metal and the walls were of rough-hewn boards with gaps between them. The door came off as Diego opened it and crashed to the ground in a cloud of dust. The sheltering rock overhang had kept the shack and the ground around it dry.

Inside, there was a single small room with a dirt floor. Bare studs held up the rough-hewn boards that formed the outside walls, and the sheet-metal roof rested directly on narrow open beams. There was no electricity, no window, and no plumbing. There was also no furniture, but a rusty old stove had once given heat.

"A great place to hide for a couple of years," Pete said. "I'd hate to live here two days!"

"You might feel differently, Second, if soldiers were chasing you, and you had a valuable sword people wanted to steal," Jupiter observed. "But I admit it's pretty bare."

"Too bare, First," Bob said. "No closets, no cupboards, no nooks, and no crannies! There's nowhere to hide anything."

"Gosh," Diego said as he looked at the bare, open walls and ceiling, "Bob's right. There's nowhere."

"The floor?" Pete suggested. "Don Sebastián could have buried the sword here, and left the spot unmarked."

Jupiter shook his head. "No, if he'd buried the sword in here, the fresh dirt would have shown for a long time.

I don't think he'd have risked that. However—"

The stocky First Investigator was looking thoughtfully at the rusted old stove. Its pipe went up through the tin roof, and its feet rested on a slab of stone.

"I wonder," Jupiter said, "if this stove can be moved easily?"

"Let's find out," Pete said.

The tall Second Investigator gave the stove a push. It was solid and heavy, but it moved. It wasn't attached to the flat stone under it.

The pipe was jointed with a short section just above the stove. "Slide up that short piece," Jupiter ordered.

Pete pushed at the short section of pipe.

"Gosh, it's rusted tight," he said.

"It wouldn't have been in 1846," Jupiter exclaimed. "Break it off if you have to."

With the help of some tools from Bob's saddlebag, Pete broke the rusty stovepipe just above the stove. Then, all together, the four boys heaved the stove off its flat slab. Pete kneeled and tried to move the stone.

"Ooofff," he grunted. "It's too heavy, First."

"Over there." Diego pointed to a wall. "That two-by-four stud looks loose."

Jupiter helped Diego to rip the two-by-four from the wall while Bob and Pete rolled the stove close to the slab. Pete dug down beside the slab until he found the bottom, then scooped out a hole big enough to let the end of the two-by-four slip under the edge of the slab. With the middle of the long stud resting against the stove as a fulcrum for their lever, the four boys heaved their weight down on the other end of the stud.

The flat stone slab flipped up and fell away, revealing a small, deep hole under it! Diego bent over the dark hole.

"I see something!" he cried even before Bob turned on his flashlight.

He reached down into the hole as far as he could and pulled out some short lengths of frayed rope, a heavy sheet of paper that was brown with age, and a long, rolled-up piece of canvas that had been tarred black. Diego looked at the browned piece of paper.

"It's in Spanish," he said. "Fellows! It's a proclamation from the U.S. Army dated September 9, 1846! Something about rules for the civilian population."

"That tarred canvas is just the size for wrapping a sword," Jupiter realized. He began to unroll the canvas with trembling hands.

"It's empty!" Pete groaned as the canvas opened on nothing.

"Diego, is there anything else down there!" Jupiter said.

Bob stood over the hole with his flashlight while Diego looked inside and felt around with his hand.

"No," Diego said, "there's nothing I . . . Wait! I've got something! It's . . . It's just a small rock."

Dejected, Diego brought his hand out and opened it to show a small, dusty rock. He rubbed it clean against his shirt. Now the small, almost square stone was a deep and glittering green!

"Is it . . . ?" Bob started to ask.

"An emerald!" Jupiter cried. "The Cortés Sword must have been in that hole! That must be where Don Sebastián had it hidden at first. When he escaped from Sergeant Brewster, he got the sword and hid it somewhere else. Maybe someone had a hint that the sword was here, or maybe he just didn't think this shack was safe enough."

"He was right," Bob said. "We spotted it pretty fast."

"Then he wouldn't have tried to hide out here himself,"

Diego said. "This can't be the place."

"No," Jupiter agreed, "but the emerald means that we're getting closer. Now we know that Don Sebastián had the sword out here. It wasn't smuggled to him. Sergeant Brewster's story has one more lie in it. No, the sword was here until Don Sebastián came for it that night and hid it somewhere else! He hid the sword, and himself, and he had to do it fast."

"Jupe?" Pete said suddenly. "What's that noise?"

They listened. It was a loud drumming sound from somewhere outside. Almost a roar like an avalanche . . .

"Rain!" Bob exclaimed. "It's hitting everywhere except here, under the rock overhang. Wow, it's a real deluge."

"No," Pete said, "I mean that other sound. Hear it?"

Jupiter shook his head and Bob shrugged. But Diego heard it.

"Voices!" Diego whispered. "Someone's out there."

They slipped out the doorway and crouched behind the thick bushes that hid the shack. The three hobolike cowboys were crossing the small canyon in the downpour. Their voices floated through the heavy rain.

". . . saw 'em come this way, Cap. Four of 'em."

". . . keep followin' this trail."

The men moved on past the shack without seeing it under the overhang, and vanished around the next hill. Jupiter stood up.

"They won't be back for a while," he said. "We'll get back to Condor Castle before they spot us. Come on."

But this time Jupiter was wrong! The boys were still crossing the open canyon when voices shouted behind them!

"You four!"

No one had to tell the boys to run!

# 16

# Mudslide!

The boys charged out of the narrow, overgrown trail into the muddy dirt road, and stopped. Breathless, they looked right and left, not knowing which way to run!

"If we run down the road," Pete said, "those cowboys might catch us before we got to the county road!"

"They'd see us if we tried to climb up on the ridge!" said Bob.

"And we can't run up the road and cross the dam," Diego added. "It's all under water—we'd be swept right over!"

Paralyzed by indecision, they boys stood on the road in the torrent of rain.

Behind them, the three pursuing cowboys crashed through the thick brush, swearing and raging as they got in each other's way. The violent voice of the black-haired Cap could be heard urging the others on.

"Hurry!" Pete cried. "Let's try the road!"

"No," Jupiter ordered. "Down in the arroyo! Toward the end of it, near the dam! They'll be sure we wouldn't try to run that way—so we will!"

Wasting no more time, the four boys plunged down into the arroyo. They clung to the side, trying to keep above the water that almost filled the deep gully. Under the cover of the steep sides and thick brush, they started to work their way toward the dam.

Up on the road heavy boots sloshed in the mud. Their hearts pounding, the boys flattened themselves against the steep bank of the arroyo, silent and motionless in the cover of thick chaparral. Three harsh voices argued angrily almost directly above them!

"Where the devil did they run!"

"Slippery little punks!"

"You think they really got the keys?"

"Sure they did! They ran, didn't they, and we couldn't find no keys at that barn!"

"Cap? Maybe they run to the dam, huh?"

"Don't be dumber than you gotta be, Tulsa. Even kids'd know better'n to try crossin' that dam now!"

"They ain't over on that ridge, so they must of took the road. Come on!"

The boots hammered and sloshed away toward the distant hacienda and the county road. In the arroyo, the boys waited, quietly in the rain.

"They're gone," Bob finally said with relief.

"We'd better go, too," Diego said. "We can't hide here."

"Only where do we go?" Pete asked. "They've got us blocked on the road, we can't cross the dam, and they'll come back this way sooner or later."

"Perhaps," Jupiter said, "there is somewhere close to the dam where we could hide until we're sure they've gone for good. And if there isn't, we'll cross that low mound and use it as cover to get to the far side of the ridge. Then we can hide behind Condor Castle. We're not safe in this arroyo. Those guys only have to look over the edge and they'll see us."

Staying close against the bank to remain hidden from the road above, the four boys made their way along the arroyo to its end. Now they could hear the water crashing over the dam on the other side of the low mound that separated the arroyo from the creek.

"Look for some space behind a rock, or a hole in the bank, or an overhang," Jupiter said.

Clinging to the sides, the boys searched the end of the arroyo with their eyes.

"Gosh, Jupe, there's no safe place to hide in this arroyo unless we get down under the water!" exclaimed Pete. "I don't even see a gopher hole!"

"Maybe there are some rocks we could hide behind on the other side of the road," said Diego, and he poked his head up out of the arroyo. "Fellows!" The slim boy leaped down against the arroyo bank. "I saw them! On the road! Those men are coming back!"

The boys all flattened themselves close to the bank of the deep arroyo. They spoke in hoarse whispers.

"Did they see us?" Bob asked.

"I don't think so," Diego said.

"Where were they on the road?" Jupiter wanted to know.

"Just about where that trail joins it," Diego whispered. "Where we came down into the arroyo."

"Maybe they'll go back to the shack," Pete said hopefully.

"No," Jupiter said grimly, "they'll come to check out the dam. We're stuck here. Let's just hope they don't decide to look in the arroyo!"

The boys strained to hear the approaching cowboys over the sound of the waterfall at the dam. Finally voices floated toward them.

". . . if we don't see 'em by the dam, I say we come back here and beat the bushes in the ditch!"

"Uh-oh! That tears it!" whispered Jupe. "We'll have to

get out of here. Look, as soon as those guys get past us and out of sight beyond the mound, we'll crawl up over the mound as fast as we can, and down the far side. Then we can get onto the ridge above the creek and take cover behind Condor Castle!"

"But, Jupe," objected Pete, "we'll be right out in the open when we're on top of the mound!"

"I know, but just for a few seconds. If we're lucky, the men won't look back before they reach the dam. By that time, we can be safe behind rocks on the ridge."

Pete shook his head at Jupe's scheme, but there was no time to think of anything better. On the road, the three cowboys were now passing the hidden boys. Their voices were still raised in argument. Jupiter cautiously peeked over the rim of the arroyo. As the cowboys disappeared out of sight beyond the mound, Jupe said, "Now!"

On their hands and knees the boys crawled out of the arroyo and up the low mound. They sank into the rain-soaked earth and pulled up bushes by their roots as they went. They felt as if every eye in the world were on their exposed backs. But there was no shout behind them as they tumbled over the crest of the mound and slid down the far side to the edge of the swollen creek.

"We made it!" Pete exulted.

"To the ridge!" Jupiter urged. "Run as low as you can!"

Bent double, they ran like crabs along the soft, slippery mound. Twice Jupiter and Bob slipped and fell sprawling, and once Diego nearly plunged into the raging creek. Plastered with mud, they ran awkwardly on with sure-footed Pete helping the others. At last the boys reached the steep, rockier slope of the high ridge.

They scrambled up toward the shelter of the great rock

of Condor Castle, dislodging showers of stones from the muddy slope.

Behind them, shouts carried above the roar of the creek!

"Cap! Over there!"

"On the ridge!"

"It's them! Get 'em!"

The boys froze on the steep slope and looked back. The three menacing cowboys had left the road and were standing close to the dam.

"They've seen us!" Diego wailed.

"And too soon!" Pete groaned.

Even as the boys watched, the three cowboys began to run across the low, soggy mound from the corner of the dam toward the ridge.

"What do we do, Jupe?" Bob cried. "They've got us cornered up here!"

"I . . . I . . . " Jupiter faltered.

A strange noise filled the air through the pouring rain and the steady surging of the creek—a roaring sound that seemed to grow louder as each second passed. It came from somewhere above the dam, from the flooding upper creek, and rushed closer and closer and closer. Halfway across the muddy mound between the dam and the ridge, the three cowboys stopped and listened, too.

"Look!" Pete yelled.

A wall of water crested ten feet above the dam!

"Something's let go upstream!" Diego cried.

Filled with brush, logs, boulders, and whole trees torn up by the roots, the massive wave poured over the dam and crashed down into the already boiling torrent of the lower creek. The whole rocky ridge on which the boys stood seemed to shudder. On the opposite bank of the creek, sliding mud carried brush and trees down into the water.

"Fellows! They're coming again!" Diego yelled.

The three cowboys were running toward them across the mound. The boys started to flee, but stopped when they saw the long mound seem to split in half below! A huge section of muddy earth slid down into the boiling creek—taking the three cowboys with it! Flailing wildly, shouting and swearing, half swimming and half hanging onto debris, the cowboys were swept downstream in the raging torrent.

"They're gone!" Bob exulted.

"Not for long," Jupiter declared. "They'll crawl out downstream, and be between us and the country road! Let's move!"

Pete led the way up the slope to the great rock of Condor Castle. They climbed up over it and started down the other side. On both sides of the ridge, mud and boulders had slid down in the heavy rain, exposing new boulders and rocky outcroppings below Condor Castle.

"Wow, the mud's sliding everywhere!" Pete exclaimed as he led the way down the steep, slippery slope.

The athletic Second Investigator leaped over a large row of exposed boulders. The others climbed up the boulders behind him—and stopped, gaping.

Pete was gone!

# 17

# The
# nest of the eagle

Pete had vanished as if the ridge itself had swallowed him up!

"Wha–what?" Diego stammered. "Where did he go?"

"Pete!" Bob cried.

"Second! Where are you?" Jupiter called frantically.

They anxiously searched the slope with their eyes, but nothing moved. Listening hard, they finally heard something. A voice that seemed to come from nowhere!

"Fellows! Down here!"

It was Pete—and his muffled voice seemed to come right out of the ridge!

"Where are you, Pete?" Diego called.

"Down here! Look right in front of those big boulders!"

The three boys jumped down in front of the exposed boulders and saw a long, narrow hole in the slope! A hole that was all but invisible until they were right on top of it! It hadn't been there before.

"A mudslide must have uncovered the hole!" Bob realized.

Jupiter bent down to the long, narrow slit in the ridge.

"Second? You need help to get out?"

"I don't want to get out!" the disembodied voice of the Second Investigator said. "It's a kind of cave, Jupe! There's loose rocks down here. We could block up the hole and those cowboys would never spot us! Come on down."

The three boys on the slope looked at each other.

"Well—" Jupiter hesitated.

"Come on!" Pete urged. "It's dry and roomy, and those guys could come back anytime!"

That reminder was all the other three needed. Bob slipped down into the narrow hole first. Jupiter followed, grunting with the effort. The stout boy stuck halfway into the narrow opening!

"I . . . I can't fit down—" he said, red-faced.

From inside the cave Bob said, "Diego, push him! We'll pull!"

Hands grabbed Jupiter's legs. Out on the slope, Diego gripped the stout leader's shoulders and pushed. With a loud sound, almost like the popping of a cork from a bottle, Jupiter slid down and vanished. Diego jumped through behind him.

Bob already had his flashlight on in the dark hole.

"Gosh!" Diego said as he looked around. "I never knew there was a cave here."

The light showed a small, rocky space about the size of a one-car garage, with a low ceiling and loose rocks and boulders strewn around the floor. The cave was still dry despite the heavy rain coming through the hole now, in the ridge. It had obviously been open only a very short time.

"Shine the light around, Records," Jupiter commanded.

The small, low cave extended back some ten or fifteen feet and ended in a pile of loose rocks that rose to the ceiling. Jupiter examined the exposed entrance and slowly nodded.

"It looks as if it was covered up sometime in the past,

fellows, probably by an earthquake. Rocks rolled down the—"

"Never mind how it got covered up," Pete exclaimed nervously. "A mudslide opened it, and those cowboys could spot the hole the same as we did! Let's block it up!"

"There's plenty of loose boulders," Diego pointed out.

The four of them rolled and heaved at the biggest rocks they could move, and finally shut out the gray light of the late afternoon. With the opening closed off, no more rain came down into the cave. The four boys sat back and grinned at each other.

"We'll wait a few hours," Jupiter decided, "and by then those cowboys should have given up and gone."

"I still wonder who they are?" Bob mused.

"They must have some connection to Mr. Norris," Diego said grimly, "or why would they have stolen Pico's hat and put it out near that campfire?"

"If they did," Jupiter said. "We only know that they were looking hard for the car keys that Bob and Pete found in the barn. I wonder why we haven't seen them with a car?"

"Well," Pete said, "they sure want those keys, so the keys must prove something bad."

"Yes," Jupiter agreed. "Perhaps they—"

"Ju–Ju–Jupe!"

It was Bob who began to stammer. He was shining his flashlight toward the pile of rocks at the rear of the cave.

"That . . . that . . . rock," Bob went on. "It's got . . . it's . . . got—"

"Eyes!" Diego gulped. "Eyes and . . . teeth!"

"A skull!" Pete moaned.

Jupiter stared at the pile of rocks. He blinked, and then

his eyes seemed to light up. He hurried toward the rear.

"It *is* a skull!" he said. "Dig around, fellows!"

Pete said unhappily, "Here's some more bones! He must have been buried in here by the quake!"

"Here's some kind of cloth under the rocks," Bob cried.

"A button!" Diego said. He held up a round piece of blackened brass. "It's a U.S. Army button!"

"This man didn't get buried in here—at least not while he was alive!" Jupiter exclaimed. "There's a hole in the skull! The guy was shot!"

The excited First Investigator looked at the others. "I think we've found the nest of the eagle! Where Don Sebastián planned to hide—and to hide the Cortés Sword! A cave right under Condor Castle would fit all the clues! And José would have known about it!"

Diego asked, "You think this soldier is one of the three who were after my great-great-grandfather?"

"I think so," Jupiter said. "And I think there must be more to this cave!"

"This pile of rock is loose," Pete said, testing it. "Maybe it blocked off part of the cave at the same time that the entrance to the cave was buried?"

Jupiter nodded in agreement.

Pete groaned. "Okay, let's start digging!"

The boys went quickly to work pulling away the fallen rocks and throwing them aside. It was long, slow work. The more rocks they pulled loose, the more rolled down to fill up the spaces. But slowly and steadily the boys inched farther ahead. The wall of loose rock grew thinner, until . . .

"I see a space!" Bob cried. He shined his flashlight ahead. "Yes! There's some kind of passage behind this pile of rocks!"

They pulled away more stones and revealed a dark, narrow passage just barely large enough for Jupiter to fit through. Holding his flashlight, Bob crawled into the dark passage first. It went straight back. A few minutes later, Bob found himself in a cavern some three times the size of the small outer chamber.

"It's a big cave!" Diego said as he crawled out of the passage and stood up.

The larger cave was about twice as high as the outer chamber, with sheer, slick sides of solid stone and a solid stone floor with a few outcroppings of rock.

"We must be right under Condor Castle," Bob guessed.

"What a place to hide!" Pete exclaimed. "You could block up the outside entrance and the passage real easy."

"With someone outside to bring in food and water," Diego added, "a man could stay in here safely for a long time."

"If he made it in here unseen, and had time to block the entrances," Jupiter said. "I don't think Don Sebastien did."

He pointed silently to the left of the passage. Bob shined his light. There was a second skeleton! It was lying on its back behind one of the outcroppings of rock. Blackened brass buttons lay around it, and there was a rusted old rifle at its side.

"He must have tried to take cover behind the rock," Pete said. "I guess it's the second of those soldiers."

"And there's the third!" Jupiter exclaimed.

Bob's light had swept ahead to reveal a third skeleton lying face down in the center of the cave. There were brass buttons lying around again, and also the remains of rotted leather boots and a crumbling leather belt with a pistol holster. A Mexican War–style revolver lay inches from the fingers of the skeleton's right hand.

"This would probably be Sergeant Brewster," Jupiter said grimly. "A pistol, and good boots." He shook his head. "No wonder the three soldiers never came back!"

"They didn't desert very far, did they?" Pete said.

"Three greedy guys looking for an easy fortune," Bob added.

"But," Diego asked, "where is my great-great-grandfather?"

Bob shined his light all around the cavern. From where they stood the boys saw nothing else. There seemed to be no hiding places in the sheer walls.

"Someone shot those three," Pete said. "If it wasn't Don Sebastián, who was it? Or did Don Sebastián just leave the cave?"

"It's possible, Second," Jupiter said thoughtfully. "But if he'd gotten all three of the soldiers, why wouldn't he just bury them and stay hidden here?"

"Maybe it wasn't Don Sebastián who shot them," Pete said. "I mean, three against one, and they were trained soldiers. Maybe there were others, and Don Sebastián didn't want—"

"It *was* Don Sebastián," Bob said. "Look over there! Way at the far end of the cave! There's another passage, and something's in it!"

When the boys reached the far wall, they saw that there wasn't a passage after all, but only a low cul-de-sac that went back in some five feet. Inside the cavity, where anyone would have been hidden from immediate view, was the fourth skeleton. It was leaning against one of the few loose boulders in the cave. The remnants of clothing were different this time. Silver *conchos* of Indian design lay near the skeleton, and by it were two rusted old rifles. Diego picked up a *concho*.

"It is of our local make," he said sadly. "I think we know now why my great-great-grandfather was never seen again. All these years he has been buried in this cave."

Jupiter nodded. "We were right all along. Don Sebastián planned to hide here. That's why he put 'Condor Castle' on the letter to José, to tell his son where he would be. He escaped from Brewster and his buddies, got his sword from the line shack, and came up here to the cave. But the soldiers followed him, and they shot it out in here. Don Sebastián had the advantage of knowing the layout of the cave. Hiding in this cul-de-sac, he could pick off the soldiers as they crawled through the narrow passage. He got all three of them, but they got him, too. Some time later an earthquake buried the cave, and no one ever knew what had happened to the four men."

"But, Jupe," said Bob, "why didn't Don Sebastián's friends come here looking for him? They knew the eagle had found a nest."

Jupiter shrugged. "We'll never know. Perhaps they didn't know exactly where he was and were awaiting further word. Or perhaps the earthquake covered the cave before they could get here. And apparently the friends were all killed or scattered in the fighting that soon broke out. By the time José got home after the war, there was no one to tell him that Sergeant Brewster's report of Don Sebastián's death wasn't true. José might not have believed that the sword fell into the ocean with his father—but he'd then assume it was simply stolen."

"Jupe!" Pete cried. "The Cortés Sword! It should be right here with Don Sebastián!"

They quickly searched the small cul-de-sac. Then they looked at each other in dismay.

There was no sword!

# 18

# The secret message

"Maybe," Bob said, "Don Sebastián hid the sword in the cave."

"In case something *did* happen to him," Diego added. "He must have known those soldiers were close behind him. The Cortés Sword was a symbol of our family as well as a treasure. He would have tried to protect the sword and save it for José."

"Let's search!" Pete cried.

With only the one flashlight the boys couldn't split up, so the search was slow work. Slow and useless. The cave was large, but there was almost no place to hide even a pin. The boys found one more little cul-de-sac and a few shallow crevices in the solid rock walls, but that was all. There were no holes in the solid stone floor, no debris to hide it under, and no place to dig and bury a sword.

"With Brewster and his cohorts close behind him, maybe on their way into the cave, I don't think Don Sebastián would have had time to hide the sword even if there were a good place," Jupiter said unhappily. "No, it looks as if he didn't have the sword with him in this cave, fellows."

"Then where is it?" Pete asked. "We're no farther along than when we started!"

Bob glumly agreed. "We've just about proven everything we guessed was true, but we still don't have any clue to where the sword is."

"I . . . I was so sure we were close to the answer," Jupiter said slowly. "We must be missing something! Think about what—"

"Jupiter?" Diego said, frowning. "If Don Sebastián wrote 'Condor Castle' on his letter to José, he knew José would come here to find him someday, right?"

"Yes, I suppose he expected to be still hiding here when José finally returned."

"But Don Sebastián got shot here instead. Now, if he didn't die right away but thought that he *was* dying, he'd worry about how José could ever find the sword. So—"

"So he would have left some message for José!" Jupiter cried "Of course! He would have been sure to try! Only after all this time would a message still be readable?"

"Depends what he wrote it on and with," Pete said. "*If* he wrote a message. I didn't see anything while we were looking."

"No," Diego admitted, "but we weren't looking for anything like a message."

"What could he have written a message with, anyway?" asked Bob. "I don't think he'd have had paper and ink with him. Not if he was on the run."

"I guess not," said Diego. "But maybe he would have written it with what he had, fellows—blood!"

"On what?" Pete said doubtfully. "If he wrote it on his shirt or something, it's long gone."

"The walls?" Bob suggested, looking around.

"Badly wounded, dying," Jupiter mused. "He couldn't have moved much. Look on the walls of that little cul-de-sac!"

They all bent low and studied the rock walls of the cavity where Don Sebastien died. His skeleton seemed to watch them from where it lay against the small boulder.

"I don't see anything," Pete said at last, staying as far from the silent skeleton as he could.

"Would blood last so long, First?" Bob wondered.

"I'm not sure," Jupiter confessed. "Maybe not."

"What's this?" Diego asked.

Near the skeleton, behind the small boulder, Diego picked up a small object that the boys hadn't seen before. It was an earthenware jug with a broken top. It looked like Indian pottery.

"It's got something at the bottom," Diego said. "Sort of black and hard."

Jupiter took the jug. "It's an Indian pot, all right. That black stuff looks like dried-up paint."

"Black paint?" Bob said.

They all looked at the pot, and then at each other.

"If he wrote something with black paint," Pete said. "It could have faded, been covered by dust, and become almost invisible!"

"Everyone dust off the walls," Jupiter said, pulling out his handkerchief. "And dust carefully! We don't want to knock off any flakes of paint!"

Working gently, they all dusted the walls of the cul-de-sac. It was Pete who finally found the faint marks.

"Bob! Shine your flashlight right over here!"

Four words stood out faintly on the stone wall to the left of the skeleton. Spanish words. Diego translated them aloud.

"Ashes . . . Dust . . . Rain . . . Ocean."

Everyone stared at the four words, wondering what they meant.

"The last two words are written pretty close together,"

Diego commented. "They're all very shaky."

"Maybe," Pete guessed, "he hid the sword in some fire-place somewhere?"

"Somewhere near the ocean?" Bob added.

"But how does 'rain' fit in?" Diego wondered.

"Maybe there's a dusty rain cistern somewhere near an outdoor fireplace," Pete said wryly. "Face it, fellows, it's gibberish! It doesn't mean anything!"

"Why would my great-great-grandfather have written something that meant nothing?" Diego demanded.

"He wouldn't have," Jupiter said. "But . . . Ashes, Dust, Rain, and Ocean?" He shook his head. "I confess I don't understand the connection at all."

"Maybe," Bob said, "Don Sebastián didn't write the words. Maybe they were written earlier by someone else."

"I don't think so, Records. Don Sebastien would have left some message for José, I'm convinced of that, and the paint was right beside him," Jupiter said. "And its unlikely that someone wrote the words after his death. If anyone had come in here later, he'd have found the four bodies and reported them, and we wouldn't have found the skele-tons. No, I'm certain that Don Sebastien wrote those words. But—?"

"Maybe he was delirious, First," Bob said. "He was hurt bad, dying. Maybe he didn't even know what he was writ-ing."

Jupiter nodded. "That's possible, yes. But, somehow, I feel the words *do* mean something, taken all together. Something that Don Sebastián knew José would under-stand. Ashes . . . Dust . . . Rain . . . Ocean."

The words seemed to echo through the hidden cave. The boys repeated them in their minds, as if hearing them over and over would reveal their secret. Concentrating hard, they were slow to notice a strange noise coming into the cave.

"Jupe!" Diego suddenly exclaimed. "What's that? That tapping noise? Up there!" He looked up toward the roof of the cave.

"Outside!" Bob said softly. "Footsteps! Someone's up on Condor Castle!"

"Maybe it's those three cowboys," Diego said.

"If it is," Jupiter said, "they won't find us. We've got the entrance to the cave blocked."

"Our tracks!" Pete said in alarm. "If they spot our tracks in the mud, they'll know we came down here! They can push those stones away from the hole if they try! Then they can—"

"Come on," Jupiter ordered.

The four boys hurried across the cave to the narrow passage and crawled back out into the smaller chamber. They crouched on either side of the blocked-up opening and waited in the dark. Soon they heard faint voices outside.

"They're coming down," Pete hissed.

The voices outside became louder, and then the boys could hear faint steps slipping and sliding down the steep ridge.

"Stay flat back against the wall on each side of the hole," Jupiter instructed. "If they do push the rocks in, and come inside, maybe they won't see us right away. When they've gone past us, we can make a dash for outside."

The sharp sound of boot heels striking stone rang above them. The voices were almost directly in front of the covered hole now! Three voices with fierce, arguing tones!

"What are they saying?" Bob whispered. "I can't make out the words."

"Neither can I," Pete whispered back.

The boys strained to hear. The angry voices seemed to be right in front of the blocked hole, yet they were oddly muffled.

"Why don't they try to come in?" Diego wondered.

"They must have seen our tracks," Pete whispered, "or why would they come straight down to the hole?"

In the dark cave the four boys waited in an agony of suspense.

"They've been out there ten minutes," Bob finally whispered.

Time seemed to stand still in the cave.

"Fifteen minutes," Bob said. "What are they—"

Boots moved out beyond the thin barrier of rocks that covered the hole! Footsteps slipped and slid—and the voices faded away! The three men were gone!

In the small cave, the boys waited another fifteen minutes.

"They didn't see the hole!" Diego exclaimed at last.

"They missed us!" Bob echoed.

"But," Pete said, "they must have followed our tracks down. How could they miss the hole? Even if it's dark out there now?"

Jupiter stared at the rocks that covered the hole. "And why couldn't we hear words? We should have been able to hear what they said if they were right outside."

For a moment, none of them spoke in the dark cave.

"Guys," Pete said at last, "pull out some of the rocks." Bob turned on his flashlight and propped it on a boulder. Then the four boys pulled out one of the large rocks they had rolled against the hole. Then they pulled out another. And a third.

There was no light or fresh air from outside.

Frantically, they removed all the rocks they had pushed into the entrance to the hidden cave.

No light, no wind, and no rain came in.

"Where is it?" Diego cried. "The entrance?"

Pete crawled into the dark space they had opened, and felt around at the end.

"Rock!" his muffled voice came back. "It's all rock!"

"You mean they blocked it up!" Bob cried, pale.

Pete crawled slowly out. His eyes were wide. "No, they didn't block it up. There's been another mudslide! A big slab of rock has slipped down over the hole. That's why those guys didn't see the hole—there isn't any hole out there now! And that's why we couldn't hear them clearly! Now what do we do? We're trapped in here!"

# 19

# Jupiter sees the light

Jupiter said quietly, "Are you sure, Second? Perhaps it's not that big a rock. Let's see if we can move it."

The four boys managed to squeeze into the narrow space of the old entrance hole. Pete counted to three, and they all heaved at the rock that had slipped across the opening.

"Ooofff!" Pete grunted.

"Owww!" Diego's feet slid out from under him and he fell.

Bob and Jupiter pushed with all their strength.

The rock didn't even move a millimeter.

"It's no use, First," Bob wailed.

"We might as well try to move the whole ridge," Pete added.

They crawled back out of the hole and sat glumly on the floor of the cave.

"There's no reason to panic," Jupiter said calmly. "Even if we can't get out right away, our families will be looking for us by tomorrow morning, and Pico can tell them about Condor Castle. We couldn't hear words, but we heard the voices out there okay, so we'll hear searchers and they'll hear us."

"Well," Bob said ruefully, "I guess our folks are kind of used to emergencies by now."

Pete groaned. "You mean we're going to stay here all night?"

"If we must," Jupiter said cheerfully. "It's not a bad cave. We're nice and dry, and there's plenty of air in here. As a matter of fact, I noticed the good air when we first came in. Since the entrance was buried a long time, there must be holes or cracks in the rock to let in air. In fact, there might be some other way out. I suggest we start looking for one right now."

"I agree with Jupiter," Diego said. "And if we keep moving, we'll stay warmer."

While Bob shined his flashlight slowly all around, Jupiter, Diego and, Pete studied the walls and ceiling of the small outer cave. They found no other way out.

"But the wall over here to the left of the blocked entrance seems to be dirt," Jupiter said, "and it's kind of damp. We might be able to dig our way out of here."

"If we had the right tools, which we don't," Pete pointed out. "Besides, the wall curves inward over there. No telling how thick it is."

Jupiter nodded. "I suggest we go back into the large cave first, and see if we can find an alternate exit."

"We searched all over in there, First," Bob objected.

"True, but let's try again. Anyway, I want to take another look at those words Don Sebastián wrote."

He led them back through the narrow passage into the cave with the skeletons. The skulls leered ominously at the boys, seeming to mock them. With Bob holding the flashlight again, the boys worked slowly all around the walls of the larger cave. There were definite currents of air from somewhere but no exits.

"I guess it's stay and wait for help," Bob said, "or dig back in the small cave."

"Some choice!" Pete moaned. "I don't want to stay, and I don't feel like digging."

"If we're going to stay all night," Jupiter said, "I suggest we put our minds to work on our puzzle. Ashes . . . Dust . . . Rain . . . Ocean."

"It's still gibberish to me," Pete said flatly.

"Unintelligible perhaps," Jupiter declared, "but I'm certain it's not gibberish. Let's take another look at the words."

In the small cul-de-sac, they squatted and looked again at the four Spanish words. Jupiter studied them thoughtfully.

"Diego was right about the four words not being evenly spaced," the stocky leader said. " 'Ashes' stands alone, and so does 'Dust,' but 'Rain' and 'Ocean' are closer together. There could even be a mark between them, sort of like a dash, as if Don Sebastián wanted them to be read together. So the message might really read: 'Ashes . . . Dust . . . Rain-Ocean.' Now what does that tell us, fellows?"

"Nothing," Pete said promptly.

Diego said, "That rain and ocean are both water?"

"Yes." Jupiter nodded. "That's one thing they are."

"Maybe that rain and ocean are really the same thing?" Bob suggested. "I mean, we know that rain really comes from water vapor rising from the ocean. It turns to water again in the sky, and falls as rain to make rivers and things."

"All right," Jupiter agreed. "The rain comes from the ocean, and then goes back to the ocean. How does that connect to dust or ashes?"

"Dust could come from ashes," Diego said. "But I guess it doesn't have to."

"Ashes don't come from dust," Pete pointed out. "No way."

"No," Jupiter said slowly. "Keep on thinking, fellows. There must be some connection, some common clue, in the four words. What single message could they all have given to José?"

None of the other boys said anything.

"Well," the stocky leader said at last, "keep trying, and meanwhile we'll go back to the small cave and see if we can dig our way out."

"We can use those old rifles for digging," Pete said.

Bob looked into his saddlebag of tools. "Not much of use in here, but we could hack at the dirt with my screwdriver."

Back in the outer cave, the boys examined the softened dirt to the left of the blocked entrance. It was damp and sticky.

"It's been raining a whole week," Pete pointed out, "and this dirt is just damp. There must be a lot of it between us and the outside. Well," he added with a grin, "let's find out!"

Using the old gun barrels, the screwdriver, and some small, flat rocks they found, the boys started to dig. At first the adobe soil was stiff and lumpy and tended to stick. Then, as the boys dug deeper, the soil got wetter. Every time they dug a foot, the heavy clay oozed back, and they had to dig faster to make any headway. And every few feet they struck rocks and boulders that had to be dug out before they could move on.

They sweated in the cave, and their faces and clothes became smeared with the heavy adobe soil. As the hours passed they grew tired and hungry. Finally they were too exhausted to keep digging. They fell asleep and didn't wake up till dawn—dawn by their watches. In the cave it was still night. The batteries in Bob's flashlight were giving out, and there wasn't much light to see by. All four boys went to work even harder than before.

It was seven-thirty when Pete cried out.

"I see light!" he yelled.

Frantically, with renewed vigor, they all plunged into the narrow hole they had made and dug like mad. The opening, and the welcome light, grew larger, and then they were through! Babbling happily, they crawled out one by one and stood in the rain on the open slope of the high ridge.

"Wow!" Pete cried, "listen to the noise!"

The violent roar of the flooded creek seemed to shake the whole countryside. Diego pointed toward the dam.

"Half the dam's collapsed!" he cried, "and—"

"The whole mound's gone now!" Bob saw.

"Look!" Jupiter exclaimed, pointing down into the arroyo.

Below them, the arroyo that went down to the hacienda a mile away wasn't an arroyo anymore. It was a deep, raging creek. The mass of water sweeping over the broken dam had washed out the mound that separated the creek from the arroyo. Now the torrent of water flowed down toward the sea not in one creek but in two!

"Gosh, the water must be running right past your hacienda now," Bob said to Diego.

On the steep slope of the ridge, Jupiter's eyes suddenly gleamed.

"Fellows!" he said, almost in wonder. "That's the answer!"

# 20

# The sword of Cortés

"What answer, First?" Pete and Bob cried.

Jupiter started to speak, but suddenly pointed along the ridge in the direction of the distant county road.

"Some men coming!" he exclaimed. "If it's those cowboys—!"

Pete shaded his eyes. Four men were running toward them along the trail through the ridges to the south—the same trail that the boys had taken to the hacienda after fighting the brush fire a week ago.

"It's my dad and Mr. Andrews!" Pete said. "They're with the sheriff and Chief Reynolds!"

The four boys ran down the ridge to meet the men.

"Pete!" Mr. Crenshaw cried. "Are you all okay?"

"We're fine, Dad," Pete said, grinning at his father.

Mr. Andrews fumed. "What were you doing out here all night!"

"We couldn't help it, Dad," Bob said, and told him about being trapped in the cave. "The mudslide opened it and then closed it on us. But we found out what happened to Don Sebastián Alvaro and those three American soldiers!"

"And solved another old mystery." Chief Reynolds smiled.

"But worried their parents half to death!" the sheriff

said sternly. "Pico Alvaro told us about your wild-goose chase trying to help save his ranch, and we've all been looking for you half the night! Your uncle, Jupiter Jones, is with his two helpers and Mr. Norris and his men, searching the other side of the creek! You had better tell us just how you got into that cave!"

"Yes, sir," Pete said. "We—"

Jupiter broke in. "We'll explain on the way to the hacienda, sir. I don't want my uncle to be worried any further. Could you radio him and the others to meet us at the burned hacienda?"

"All right, but you had better have a good story. I can't have reckless boys running loose in my back country!"

The sheriff used his walkie-talkie to instruct everyone to meet at the Alvaro hacienda, and the boys told their story as they walked down the trail through the ridges. They described their search for the sword and their troubles with the three cowboys. By the time they had finished, the group had reached the county road, crossed the bridge over the former arroyo, and arrived at the hacienda.

Uncle Titus, with Hans and Hans's brother, Konrad, was already there. Behind him, Mr. Norris stood near the Norris ranch wagon with Skinny, the manager Cody, and two other men.

A deputy sheriff waited in the sheriff's car. Uncle Titus hurried up to Jupiter. "Jupiter? Are you all right? Is everyone?"

"We're all okay, Uncle Titus."

Skinny walked up with Mr. Norris and Cody.

"Boy, how dumb can you guys get?" Skinny sneered.

"That's enough, Skinner," Mr. Norris snapped. "I'm glad you're all safe, boys."

"Now tell us," the sheriff said, "why were those three men chasing you?"

"Because they framed Pico for starting the brush fire," Pete said eagerly, "and maybe burned the hacienda!"

Cody snorted. "Alvaro started the fire. He's too irresponsible to own a ranch around here."

"After tomorrow he won't." Skinny laughed.

Mr. Norris snapped, "I told you to be quiet, Skinner! You too, Cody." He looked at Jupiter. "Can you prove that Pico Alvaro didn't cause the brush fire, Jones?"

"We know he didn't, Mr. Norris," Jupiter said. "Pico had his hat at three P.M. that day, when he was with us at the central school. Since the sheriff has said that the campfire was started before three P.M., Pico couldn't have lost his hat at that campfire."

Bob put in, "Skinny—I mean Skinner, sir, and Mr. Cody must have seen Pico wearing the hat at school, too!"

"I don't remember him wearing any hat," Skinny said.

"Because he wasn't," Cody added.

"He was, sir," Jupiter said firmly. "And he had it on when we arrived at the hacienda later that afternoon. He hung it on a peg in the barn, and when the brush fire started he ran out and left it. It should have burned with the barn, but it didn't. Those three cowboys came to the barn while everyone was at the brush fire, stole the hat, and put it near that campfire to frame Pico."

"You can't prove that," Cody growled. "Why would those cowboys frame Alvaro—if there even are any cowboys?"

Jupiter ignored the manager. "They framed Pico because *they* really built that illegal campfire. I'm pretty sure they burned the barn and hacienda, too."

"*Can* you prove it, Jupiter?" Chief Reynolds asked.

"And where do we find these cowboys?" the sheriff said.

"I think you can find them on the Norris ranch."

Mr. Norris said angrily, "Are you saying that I'm involved with those men and what they may have done, young man?"

"No, sir, I don't think you knew anything about them. But someone here did and does. They didn't go to the Alvaro barn alone to get the hat, did they, Skinny?"

"Skinner?" Mr. Norris stared at his son.

"He's crazy, Dad!" Skinny cried.

Jupiter reached into his pocket, and held up the set of car keys. "We found these keys in the barn. Those cowboys were looking for them, and that's why they were chasing us—to get the keys. The keys were dropped when Pico's hat was taken. I think you'll find that they belong to the Norris ranch wagon!"

"Our wagon?" Mr. Norris cried.

"I'm sure of it, sir," Jupiter said. "I'll try them, or maybe Skinner will show us his set so we can compare."

"Skinner?" Mr. Norris stared at his son again.

"I—I—" Skinny stammered, and suddenly glared at Cody. "I gave them to Cody, Dad! He told me he lost his at the brush fire! He didn't tell me—"

"You rotten coward!" Cody raged. "Okay, the keys are my set to the ranch wagon. I dropped them in that barn getting the Mex's hat, and Skinny knew all about it!"

Everyone looked at the stocky ranch manager.

"Those dumb cowboys are friends of mine," the manager said angrily. "They're in trouble, and I owed 'em a favor, so they came to me. I let them camp and hide out on Mr. Norris's place. The idiots built campfires when I told 'em not to, and got the brush fire started. I knew if

Mr. Norris found out the truth he'd fire me, so we went to the Alvaro place and I spotted Pico's hat in the barn. We took it, and put it out near the campfire later. Only I dropped my lousy keys in the barn!"

The sheriff said grimly, "Why didn't you look for them then?"

"I was in a hurry to plant the hat," Cody said uneasily, "and we were afraid of being spotted, and—"

"And the barn was already on fire, I'll bet!" Pete cried.

"Yeh," Cody said miserably. "It wasn't me, you know? I didn't mean to cause any damage, or hurt anyone. I just wanted to keep Mr. Norris from finding out about Cap, Pike, and Tulsa camping on his land and starting that brush fire. But those stupid saddle-tramps heard me say we wanted the Alvaro ranch and thought they were helping me by setting the barn and hacienda on fire! I didn't know until too late, and my keys were inside the barn!"

"You sure know you've been trying to stop us from helping the Alvaros," Bob said angrily. "You and Skinny! Snooping, listening at windows, trying to scare us!"

"That was just doing my job!" Cody protested.

"A job," Mr. Norris snapped, "you no longer have! Go and get your belongings, Cody. You're through as of now!" He glared at Skinny. "I'll talk to you later, young man!"

"He can get his things," the sheriff said, "but my deputy will go with him. He's under arrest for framing Pico Alvaro, and maybe for arson, too."

The sheriff and his deputy took Cody away to their car. Mr. Norris ordered Skinny to the ranch wagon and faced the boys.

"I want the Alvaro ranch, and I'm going to get it," he said bluntly. "But I never intended to get it by dishonesty. I'm sorry."

Before Chief Reynolds went to his car, he smiled.

"You've cleared an innocent man, boys. Pico will be released from jail immediately. Well done!"

As everyone else left the hacienda yard, Uncle Titus looked at his watch and told Hans and Konrad to bring up the salvage-yard truck.

"It's time you four got cleaned up and had some food," he said to the Investigators and Diego. "Then we'll see if you're in shape to go to school."

"But first we must remain out here another fifteen minutes," Jupiter said. "I think that's just time enough."

"Stay out here?" Uncle Titus said, puzzled. "Why, Jupiter?"

"Time enough for what, First?" Bob said.

"Why, to stop Mr. Norris from getting the Alvaro ranch, of course," Jupiter said a little pompously. "To find the Cortés Sword!"

"I forgot!" Diego cried. "You said you had the answer."

"And I do," Jupiter proclaimed. "Follow me."

He walked toward the county road with the boys and Uncle Titus behind him. The rain had stopped, and the morning sun was trying to break through the clouds. As the group neared the bridge over the arroyo, Jupiter stopped.

"Do you remember that entry in the American lieutenant's journal? The one that said he'd seen Don Sebastián on a ridge across the creek with a horse and a sword?"

"Sure," Pete said. "The entry that was all wrong, because coming from the hacienda there isn't any ridge across the creek."

"There is now," Jupiter said triumphantly, "and there was in 1846. Look!"

Beyond the arroyo, which was now a raging creek, the

statue of the headless horse stood out clearly on its high ridge!

"In 1846 and before," Jupiter reasoned, "there must have been two branches of Santa Inez Creek. We couldn't tell that on the old maps we saw because an arroyo and a creek look the same on a map. But in 1846, when the lieutenant was here, the arroyo was a creek, too. At some point, a landslide on the ridge by the old dam formed that mound and blocked off one branch of the creek. Maybe the same earthquake that buried the cave caused the landslide, too. Anyway, half the creek became an arroyo, and its been dry ever since. Everyone forgot that it ever had been a creek."

"So that lieutenant was right!" said Bob. "He did see Don Sebastián on a ridge across Santa Inez Creek. He saw him at the statue, and thought it was a real horse because he was a stranger and didn't know about the statue!"

"Exactly, Records."

Jupiter led the others across the bridge and started to climb the steep ridge. Pete stared up at the headless horse standing against the now clearing sky.

"Don Sebastián must have been hiding the sword cover when that lieutenant saw him," the Second Investigator said. "So you think there's some clue we missed at the statue, First?"

"Ashes . . . Dust . . . Rain-Ocean," the stout leader of the team intoned. "I was convinced it was Don Sebastián's last message to his son José, and it was! Think, fellows! The rain comes from the ocean, and goes back to the ocean in the end. What do ashes go back to? What does dust go back to? They were very religious people, the Spanish Californians. They—"

"Ashes to ashes!" Diego cried.

"And dust to dust," Bob echoed. "The phrase from the church's burial service! It means that in the end everything goes back to where it came from. Where it began!"

"Yes!" Jupiter crowed. "Don Sebastián, badly wounded, had only a short time. He wrote a clue he was sure José would understand at once. He knew José would realize that he had tried to save the sword from the Americans, and wrote those four words to tell José where it was— back where it had begun. With Cortés himself!"

Reaching the top of the ridge, they all looked at the headless horse with its bearded wooden rider proudly staring out over the Alvaro land.

"You mean," Uncle Titus said, "that the sword is hidden in the statue after all? Just like the cover?"

"But we searched the statue," Diego protested. "There isn't anywhere to hide a sword!"

"Don't say he buried it!" Pete groaned. "I've had more digging than I want for another hundred years!"

"No, Second," Jupiter said, "I don't think any digging will be necessary. Remember how we wondered from the start about why Don Sebastián would separate the sword from its leather cover? The cover protected the valuable sword, yet for some reason he separated them. Well, now I know the reason!"

"Why, Jupe!"

"Tell us!"

"Where is the sword, First!"

Jupiter grinned. "Remember that pot of black paint in the cave that Don Sebastián wrote the message with? Well, he used that paint for something else, too. He really returned the sword to where it had started. It's not hidden *in* the statue, it's hidden *on* the statue!"

The stout leader reached up and pulled at the wooden

sword hanging at the side of the wooden figure of Cortés. It came off in his hands with a ripping of nails, and as it hit the side of the headless horse it clanged! Jupiter took out his pocket knife and scraped at the black surface of the scabbard just as a dazzling sun broke through the clouds.

Where Jupiter had scraped, a long row of gems glowed red and blue and green and diamond white against silver metal!

"The Cortés Sword," Jupiter said, holding it up to the sun.

# 21

# Alfred Hitchcock sees justice triumph

"Ashes to ashes, and dust to dust," Alfred Hitchcock intoned. "A brilliant message by Don Sebastián, my young friends, and an even more brilliant deduction by our brainy Jupiter!"

The boys were in the comfortable office of the famous motion-picture director some days later. They had come to report on their latest case and to ask if Mr. Hitchcock would provide an introduction to Bob's written account of it. With the boys was an armed guard, for they had brought the Cortés Sword to show Mr. Hitchcock. It lay on the director's desk with all the black paint now removed. It was a dazzling display of gold, silver and jewels. Jupiter pointed out one of the emeralds. It was the stone that the boys had found in the line shack, now safely back in place on the sword.

"A most rare treasure indeed." Mr. Hitchcock almost purred as he touched the fabulous sword with more than a hint of envy. "So the Alvaros are saved, and what of those who caused all the trouble and harm?"

"The sheriff caught those three cowboys back in the hills on the Norris ranch, as I expected," Jupiter said. "It seems they were hiding out there with Cody's help because they were wanted in Texas for robbery. They admitted setting the hacienda fire, so Cody is free of the charge."

"Does the rascally Cody go free?" the director demanded.

"No, sir," Bob said. "He's charged with various felonies for framing Pico, harboring fugitives, and loosing his dogs at us. Just to name some of the charges!"

"Ah," Mr. Hitchcock said with satisfaction. "It appears he will not be worrying about keeping a job for some time to come."

"Of course," Pete added, "Skinny got off with almost nothing. He didn't really do anything except keep silent about what Cody and the three cowboys had done. His father's lawyers blamed it all on Cody's bad influence and got him probation. Mr. Norris has already sent him out of the state to military school!"

"I fear that young Skinner's poor behavior stems from an overindulgent parent," the director said with a sigh. "Let us hope that it's not too late for the military school to help! But now, what will happen to the Cortés Sword?"

"Well," Jupiter said with a grin, "when Mr. Norris saw it, he offered to buy it himself!"

"For less money than anyone else offered, of course," Bob added. "I guess Mr. Norris just can't help being greedy."

"A local bank has loaned Pico and Diego the money to pay off the mortgage to Mr. Norris at once, so they don't have to decide what to do with the sword right away."

"Generous of them." Mr. Hitchcock snorted. "Thunderation! Bankers are like patrons of the arts—they give you money when you no longer need it!"

"Anyway," Pete said, "Pico and Diego have just about decided to sell the sword to the Mexican Government for their National Museum of History, even though that's not the highest offer. Pico says the sword really belongs to the history of Mexico and the Alvaro family."

"A proud and honorable decision," the great film maker said.

"The Mexican Government is still going to pay more than enough for the Alvaros to pay off their loan, rebuild the hacienda, and buy more farm equipment," Jupiter said, and he smiled. "And enough for *them* to buy *Mr. Norris's* ranch, too!"

Mr. Hitchcock gaped. "You mean the arrogant Norris has abandoned his attempt to be a land baron?"

"Yes, sir." Pete laughed. "It seems that Pico could sue him for big damages for what Cody did in his employ! When Mr. Norris heard that, he fell all over himself offering to sell his land to the Alvaros at a very low price—if they agreed not to sue!"

"And Pico and Diego may even be able to buy back more of the old Alvaro land grant," Bob added.

The famous director roared with laughter.

"Magnificent!" he boomed. "The tables are neatly turned! Sometimes it seems that justice really does triumph! This is one case I shall insist on introducing!"

The boys thanked him, and left with the sword and the guard. Mr. Hitchcock sat smiling as they departed. Justice had indeed been well served in the case of the Headless Horse, and, the famous director had no doubt, would be again in the next adventure of The Three Investigators!

ALFRED HITCHCOCK and the
Three Investigators Series